# Sugar Pine Cowboy

Stephanie Berget

The characters and events in this book are fictitious. Any similarity to real persons, living or dead, places, or events is coincidental and not intended by the author.

If you purchase this book without a cover you should be aware that this book may have been stolen property and reported as "unsold and destroyed" to the publisher. In such case the author has not received any payment for this "stripped book."

Sugar Pine Cowboy
Copyright © 2018 Stephanie Berget
All rights reserved.

This book, or parts thereof, may not be reproduced in any form without permission. The copying, scanning, uploading, and distribution of this book via the internet or via any other means without the permission of the publisher is illegal and punishable by law. Please purchase only authorized electronic or print editions, and do not participate in or encourage piracy of copyrighted materials. Your support of the author's rights is appreciated.

# Other Titles by Stephanie Berget

### *Sugar Coated Cowboys*

Gimme Some Sugar

Sweet Cowboy Kisses

Cowboy's Sweetheart

### *Rodeo Road*

Changing A Cowboy's Tune

### *Change of Heart Cowboys*

Radio Rose

STEPHANIE BERGET

# DEDICATION

To those special men who came into our lives, showed us what it meant to be a cowboy then left us all too soon.

STEPHANIE BERGET

# CHAPTER ONE

Marlene Clegg pushed the pile of wrinkled, one-dollar bills across the counter and frowned at the young man behind the cash register. "I only pumped seven dollars worth of gas. Go check if you don't believe me."

The kid couldn't have been over sixteen. With dark hair and clear blue eyes, he had the youthful good looks she'd have gone for in high school. But her high school days were far past.

The kid walked to the window and glanced out at the pump. With a nod, he hurried back to where she stood, snatched up the money, and shoved it into the register, never taking his gaze off her.

She finger-combed her curly hair into a ponytail then let it drop back to her shoulders. In spite of her best efforts to appear self-assured a traitorous sigh broke free. She'd known it would be hard coming back to her hometown. She'd thought she could handle the animosity from Micah's friends. She'd assumed the good people of East Hope would forget, but if even the high school kid at the co-op hated her, she hadn't figured right.

Since the moment she'd set foot back in her hometown, every person in town had given her dirty looks or turned away, pretending she didn't exist. Not without cause, she'd earned her reputation, but she'd hoped someone would give her a chance. She pulled in a deep breath and attempted a smile. "Can I get a receipt, please?"

The East Hope Co-op's employee stared at her for another minute then grabbed the crumpled ticket, smoothed it out on the counter, and handed it to her. "Can I help you with anything else, Mrs. West?"

His words were polite, but from the look on his face, he was sure she was about to grow horns and attempt to eat him.

"No, thank you, and I'm not Mrs. West any more. My name is Clegg." A shudder ran up her body as she said the word. The sound of her last name was so white trash, but taking back her maiden name was part of the penance she'd forced herself to pay for her past sins.

She gave the kid a smile, slid the handle of her purse over her shoulder, and walked out with as much dignity as she could manage. This was not the way she'd envisioned her homecoming. Her long imagined reappearance had been filled with money, an expensive sports car, and fabulous shoes.

She glanced at her ancient pick-up then down to her scuffed, black Danskin slip-ons. Not exactly what she'd had in mind. Her gran had always told her to dream big, and the dream included a drive down Main Street in a Lamborghini.

The mental picture of the top-of-the-line sports car next to her truck made her wince. The boxy shape of her '87 Chevy pickup looked more like a railroad car than a sexy speedster.

With everything she owned piled in the back, she only needed to add a rocking chair to be the Beverly Hillbillies' long lost cousin. Orange paint had chipped off the sides in a haphazard pattern, and she'd replaced the missing tailgate with a rope. The worst part was the damned thing sucked fuel like it was dying of thirst, but she'd spent the last of her meager savings to buy it, and it ran. Most of the time.

She slid into the seat and turned the key. With a groan and a belch of smoke, the engine caught. Only one more stop before she could leave town and head out to Uncle Jeb's place. She'd cut out a lot of things from her life, but she still had to eat, and the only place within forty miles was Foodtown. If she was lucky, and she usually wasn't, the owner would be out.

She drove the few blocks from the Co-op to the grocery store and parked in front. The butterflies in her stomach did backflips on top of pirouettes. The interaction at the co-op had been bad enough, but this had the potential to be catastrophic.

Well, what did she expect? She'd made her reputation in this town, and now she had to live with it.

Marlene slid out of the truck, kept her head down, and walked through the front door. Without looking right or left, she grabbed the cart. Keeping a tally of the prices in her head, she picked up the essentials. Coffee was the only optional thing she wasn't willing to do without—yet. She put the can in the cart and looked around. Only half way through the store and she'd hit her spending limit. Time to get out of here before Millie showed up.

As she stood at the checkout counter, talking to a girl she didn't know, she thought she had it made. She opened her wallet, and thumbed through the few remaining bills.

Quick footsteps thudded closer on the old vinyl floor, and she turned to see Millie Barnes, the owner and a spiteful adversary.

"What are you doing here?" The storeowner's voice boomed through the room, loud and accusatory.

Marlene ignored Millie and tried to hand the checkout girl enough money to cover the groceries.

The girl stood motionless, her eyes wide, shifting between the two women.

Marlene laid the money on the counter, picked up the plastic bags, and turned slowly, preparing for the confrontation.

Millie looked exactly as she had when Marlene last saw her, fiery red hair, jeans and boots and an on-the-warpath expression. "Hi, Millie. You haven't aged a day since I saw you a couple of years ago." The pleasant words wouldn't do her any good, but she'd made up her mind to try.

Millie placed her hands on her hips and stepped forward until her crimson bouffant almost touched Marlene's forehead.

In her previous life, Marlene had never backed down from anyone. Now, she had the urge to turn and run. Being a nice person was harder than it looked.

"Didn't Micah pay you enough? You promised to stay away. No one wants you here." Millie's eyes narrowed. Her hands fisted.

For a second Marlene thought the older woman was going to hit her. She forced a smile, and allowed herself to take one step back. "I'm here to clean up Uncle Jeb's farm and sell it. Want to help?" Why did her brain take leave of her senses? The words were guaranteed to infuriate Millie, and from the glare she got, they'd worked. "Guess not.

She turned and hurried toward the door. As it swung shut behind her, she heard the shrill voice once more. "I can't keep you out of East Hope, but I can keep you out of my store. Buy your food someplace else."

So much for hoping the good folks of East Hope had forgiven her.

Climbing into the dilapidated truck, she took a minute to catch her breath. It would be a relief to get out to Jeb's farm and away from town. She turned the key, and the usually trustworthy vehicle refused to start.

Dropping her head to the steering wheel, she pulled in a deep breath and steadied herself. Marlene Clegg didn't cry, especially where someone could see her.

What was she going to do if her truck didn't start? Everyone in this town hated her. There wasn't a soul she could call to help. Even if she had a friend in town, she couldn't afford a cell phone to make the call.

Marlene twisted the key again with no results. A third try and the engine groaned in protest as the truck's motor caught. A sigh of relief coursed through her. Disaster averted again, barely.

Without a backward glance, she drove out of town toward the farm she'd inherited from her great uncle. She was almost afraid of what she'd find. She hadn't seen Uncle Jeb for several years.

She'd walked away from her uncle when she'd left East Hope to find a better life. Now she wished she'd kept in touch. Jeb had been the only person in her life who'd seen beneath the party girl exterior she'd perfected.

Six weeks ago, she'd gotten a phone call out of the blue. The memory of Jeb's gravely voice washed over her, and her throat closed with tears. Uncle Jeb had told her he was fine. He'd told her he was feeling better. He'd told her not to worry, so she hadn't.

If she'd listened harder maybe she could have picked out the lie, but she'd been too busy trying to keep her head above water.

One memory gave her a bit of peace. Uncle Jeb had always sworn he wanted to drop dead doing something he loved, and besides horses, he'd loved plants. The neighbor had found him face down in his garden, a seedling in one hand, a spade in the other. She guessed he'd gotten his wish.

Marlene slowed and turned into the narrow driveway leading to Jeb's house. She pulled to a stop in back of the dilapidated mobile home. A shudder ran down her spine. The screen door hung at a crooked angle and the torn window screens fluttered in the wind. A chicken and her chicks pecked their way across the dried grass of the front yard, and a stray cat raced for the woodpile.

Home, sweet, home.

The thought of spiders and mouse droppings caused Marlene to hesitate. Turning in the seat, she looked back down the driveway. If she left right now, she could be . . . Where? She'd give anything to have somewhere else to stay, but she didn't. She'd burned all her bridges trying to be someone she wasn't.

She straightened and grabbed the bags of cleaning supplies and climbed out of the truck. The food would be safer in the cab for the time being.

As she waded through the overgrown lawn something moved. A small garter snake wiggled its way through the dry stalks and past the toes of her shoes. Before she could react, a flash of feathers flew across her feet. The baby snake searched for a hiding place as the hen pecked the crap out of it.

Marlene gently pushed the hen out of the way with her foot and gave the little snake time to get away.

She'd retained enough country-girl to know garter snakes did a lot of good. Their diet consisted of almost anything they could catch, including rodents and bugs, and one look told her there was enough of each to last a lifetime on this place.

The snake slid beneath a gnarled root of the giant Sugar Pine in the back yard.

Uncle Jeb had transplanted the tree the year Great Aunt Mary died. Everyone said it wouldn't live at this altitude, but he'd nursed it along. It was still here, tall and healthy, forty years later. Marlene stood beneath the thick boughs and looked up at the clusters of narrow pinecones clinging to the ends of the branches.

To say Uncle Jeb had a green thumb was an understatement. He was a genius with plants, and the Sugar Pine was another one of his gardening miracles.

Marlene pulled herself from the memories and turned toward the mobile home. What had she gotten herself into? Not that she'd had much of a choice. Her only other option had been one she'd never be desperate enough to do—sell her body.

She tested each step of the sagging porch to make sure

they would hold her weight. The weathered boards groaned, but didn't give way as she reached the back door. She fished out the key she'd received from Uncle Jeb's attorney, but when she tried to fit it into the lock, the door gave way and swung open.

Had someone broken in? She looked around, but decided no one in their right mind would break into a dump like this. The only reason she was here was because she had nowhere else to go.

The door stuck against the floor when it was halfway open, and she put her shoulder against it. When it gave way with no warning, she landed face down on the worn linoleum of the entryway.

As she lay there, she heard a soft giggle.

A young girl peered around the kitchen wall, her eyes a startling blue, her skin freckled and her hair as red as Marlene's. Two barrettes, the same color as her eyes, held the sides away from her face.

"Are you going to invite me in?" Marlene pushed herself into a sitting position. She brushed dry grass clippings and crushed leaves off her sweater and snuck another look at the girl. Ten to twelve was Marlene's guess.

"Seems like you're already in." The girl giggled again as Marlene picked part of a candy wrapper out of her hair. "You live here?"

"I do now." Marlene gathered the scattered cleaning supplies and carried them into the kitchen. The countertops, appliances, and even the worn linoleum were surprisingly clean in comparison to the rest of the place.

The girl stood her ground, an uncertain look on her face. A lock of her string-straight hair had worked its way out of her barrette and fallen across her eyes.

"What are you doing in here?" Marlene stopped in front of her.

The girl pulled herself up to her less than five-foot height. She looked Marlene in the eye. "I always come in on Wednesdays to water Jeb's plants. Just 'cause he's dead don't mean the plants have to die."

"Doesn't mean," Marlene corrected, before realizing she now sounded like her gran. She turned and looked around the room. Other than the avocado shag carpet, there wasn't a green thing in sight. "Where are these plants you're talking about?"

The girl gestured with her arm, and started down the hall. "Follow me." Fishing a key out of her pocket, the tiny redhead opened a padlock on one of the bedroom doors, swung the hasp open and stepped back to allow Marlene to enter.

Light filled the small room. Equipment lined one wall. Lush plants grew beneath grow lamps, the bright green leaves fairly glowing in the artificial light. Marlene counted four large plants and several smaller ones. "This is marijuana!" She turned and stared at the girl.

"Course it is. Jeb couldn't make any money growing roses." The kid picked up a watering can, filled a pitcher to the black line drawn on the side and gently watered the nearest plant. She checked the leaves then moved on to the next one.

Marlene stood frozen in amazement.

Her ninety-three year old great uncle had been a pothead!

\*~\*

The seat and floorboards of Bose Kovac's three-quarter ton Dodge pickup were strewn with papers, coffee cups and burger wrappers. He normally kept the truck cleaner than his house, but he'd been at a horseshoeing seminar in Sacramento for the last three weeks. "Tomorrow this gets cleaned out no matter what emergency comes up." He knew it was an empty promise. Horses came first, and if one needed him, he'd be there.

The fuel pump clicked off, and he returned the nozzle to its place. He was done shoeing for the day, and it wasn't a moment too soon. The ranchers, team ropers, barrel racers and hobby riders in this area had been hauling to Burns to get their horses shod since old Jeb Clegg had thrown out his back and retired six months ago. They were anxious to see what kind of farrier had moved into the community. And they all had emergencies.

The thought of Jeb reminded him he needed to check in on the old man. When he'd taken off for the seminar, he'd left a message on his phone to get ahold of Jeb in case of a shoeing emergency.

When his old friend hadn't called, Bose assumed everything had gone well, but it wouldn't hurt to stop by and make sure. He turned down the country road leading to Jeb's home. If he put off the visit, there was no telling how long it would be before he'd have time again.

The doublewide sat in the center of forty acres, and as Bose turned into the driveway, he saw a rusty, orange truck speed around a corner of the house and head toward the driveway.

The truck wasn't Jeb's.

The lane was only wide enough for a single vehicle, and since he was suspicious of any stranger racing away from his friend's place, he stopped in the middle, blocking the way out. As he climbed out a panicked redhead jumped out of the other vehicle.

"You've got to come help me! Jeb's crazy horse is caught in the fence." She ran back to her truck, but stopped when he didn't move.

"Marlene?" He couldn't believe his eyes. Curly red hair floated in a halo around her head, and her body still did great things to a pair of jeans. She was a few years older but still beautiful. He slammed his eyes shut before opening them slowly.

Standing in front of him was the woman he'd hoped to never see again.

Her sharp voice chased away all doubts. "Get a move on," she shouted, slammed the old truck into reverse, and sped backwards down the drive.

Bose shook his head and climbed back into his truck. There was no one in this world he'd rather avoid than Marlene Clegg. He wouldn't have gone anywhere near Jeb's place if he'd known the old man's great niece was back in town. Bose parked the truck and hurried around the mobile home to the barn.

Marlene waited a little way down the fence from where Jeb's four-year-old roan colt stood. The animal held one leg held out in front at an odd angle.

Bose walked slowly toward the young horse crooning as he got closer. "Hey there, Louie. What have you gotten yourself into now?" Sweat darkened the animal's coat and his eyes were rimmed with white.

Marlene kept her mouth shut, for which he was grateful. The colt didn't need someone yelling and upsetting him more than he already was.

"Easy, buddy. I've got you." Bose eased up beside the colt. "Easy now little Louie.

The young gelding had pawed at the fence, probably trying to get to a morsel of grass on the other side, and wedged the bottom strand of wire between his shoe and his hoof.

Bose leaned down, thankful Jeb had done a lot of groundwork with this colt. He looked at Marlene, watching from a safe distance. "Go to my truck and get the wire cutters out of my tool box. Now!"

She turned and walked slowly until she was a few yards away then ran. She'd gotten smarter in the ten years since he'd seen her last, not that it made any difference. Smart didn't equal kind.

Bose stroked the colt's neck. The old horseshoer had always had an eye for good horses, and this one was no exception. The animal was scared, but he stood still for the moment. The well built blue roan Jeb called Louie Blues was an eye-catcher. The gelding was gentle, but needed a lot of riding. Just the kind of horse Bose would have bought if he'd had a place of his own, but he was renting a trailer behind a farmhouse on the edge of town. Until he found a place to buy, horses were out.

Marlene appeared around the edge of the house, the nippers held in front of her as she ran.

Bose held up a hand to slow her down. They didn't need the horse panicking and pulling back. He'd already worked up a sweat trying to escape.

She nodded and slowed to a walk, her voice barely above a whisper. "Is he okay? I came out to clean up the backyard and found him like this."

"Where's Jeb?" An old rope halter, stiff with dirt and sweat, lay on the ground outside the fence. He eased it on the colt.

She cocked her head, and her brows drew down. "He's gone."

The colt must have decided it had had enough of the chitchat. He tensed and leaned his weight against the wire, on the verge of panic.

Bose eased his hand into the halter and talked to Louie. It wouldn't do for Jeb's colt to hurt himself. "Hand me the cutters slow and easy." Taking the tool from Marlene, he cut one side of the wire.

The colt danced away until the wire was tight again. He gave a soft snort and leaned against the pressure.

Bose stroked his neck. "Easy now, buddy. Let me fix this." He reached across and clipped the other side of the wire freeing the animal.

The colt almost fell backward until he realized he was free. He gave a big sigh and stepped closer to Bose.

Marlene watched, her face pale. "What do we do now?"

Bose picked up the colt's foot and tried to ease the wire from beneath the shoe. It was stuck tight. "I'll take him out to my truck and pull this shoe."

Marlene followed them to the front of the house, keeping her distance from both Bose and the colt.

It only took a few minutes to fix the pull the shoe. He

kept his attention on the job of resetting it. When he'd finished, he held the lead rope out to Marlene, determined to get away from her as soon as he could. Even after all these years he could feel the pull of her personality. He wasn't about to get sucked into her chaos-filled world again.

She put her hands in the pockets of her denim capris and backed away. "You take him."

He looked into the unusual eyes he remembered so well. They were electric blue rimmed in navy with a gold ring next to her pupils. He'd been mesmerized by them when he'd first met her. She'd once been his whole world. He remembered thinking if he could look into Marlene's eyes every day, nothing would be too tough to handle. Little did he know, she'd be the one to break him.

"Turn him back into the pasture." He held out the lead rope and took a step toward her. "I've got things to do."

She shook her head and moved away to sit on the porch. "Can you put him away, please?"

There was a day this helpless act could have gotten him to do anything she asked. That day was gone. He tied the horse to the pole fence surrounding the property, and turned toward his truck.

"Wait!" Marlene hurried toward him. "Remember, I'm afraid of horses."

Bose remembered a lot of things. "The post is solid. The horse will be fine until Jeb gets home." He climbed into the cab of his truck, but as he pulled on the door, Marlene grabbed the handle and held it open.

"You haven't heard?"

If he hadn't known better, he would have thought he saw tears fill her eyes. If they were there, they were manufactured to get what she wanted. No use even answering. He wasn't going to be drawn into more of Marlene's drama. He turned the key. He could drive away with the door open.

"Boris, please."

# SUGAR PINE COWBOY

A frisson of shock ran down his spine. No one used his given name. Not since Marlene had dumped him. He'd been Bose since his little cousin, Atlas, had butchered his name when he was three. His jaw muscles tightened, and tension pulled his shoulders nearly to his ears. Was he going to have to run her over to get away?

Flicking off the ignition, he climbed out and untied the horse.

The tired gelding sniffed Bose's shirt. Satisfied, he dropped his head and began to graze.

He could see Marlene watching him from the porch, her eyes wide, her arms crossed. "Thank you, Boris."

"That's enough, Marlene." Bose jiggled the lead rope until the blue roan raised his head then led the horse back to the pasture. The gelding nickered to the other horse in the pasture and trotted off to join his buddy.

When Bose turned around, Marlene stood right behind him. "I need to talk to you."

The memory of the soft hands that went along with her soft voice almost stopped him, but she'd always used her considerable assets to get what she wanted. He wasn't falling for her act again. "We said everything we needed to say years ago." He stepped around her and started toward the front yard.

Marlene hurried to catch up and laid her hand on his arm. "Really, Bose. I need to tell you something. Let's sit on the porch."

He shifted so she wasn't touching him. "All right, Marlene. Say what you have to. Like I said before, I'm busy." He was actually on his way home, but she didn't need to know that.

Marlene drifted over to the porch and sat down, patting on the step beside her. "This is important."

This woman was the most stubborn person on the face of the earth. He had no doubt she'd follow him home if he didn't at least give her a few minutes. He dropped into a rickety wooden lawn chair as far from her as he could get.

"Have your say."

"There's a reason I couldn't leave the horse tied to the fence until Uncle Jeb came home." She looked away from him, her gaze fixed on the treetops. "Uncle Jeb isn't coming home. He died a week ago."

# CHAPTER TWO

Marlene grabbed another fist full of Bindweed and pulled only to have the weed snap off at ground level. It would grow back before she made it all the way down the back of the trailer. As she threw the stems into the rusty wheelbarrow, her glove came off with them.

The only gloves she'd been able to find had been Uncle Jeb's, and they were several sizes too big and stiff with dirt and age.

She'd seen some cute, purple edged, woman sized ones in the co-op, but they'd been seven dollars, and she didn't have a quarter to spare. With a lot of work and a ton of swearing, she'd managed to mow the lawn with Jeb's old push mower, and the next job on her list was weeding along the back of the house.

The last time she'd been here, over three years ago, the yard had been in perfect shape and the flowerbeds immaculate. She'd been surprised to find the place in disrepair. She turned at the sound of hooves beating against the pasture.

The blue roan was feeling his oats this morning, racing from one end of the pasture to the other. The second horse, a brown one, stood in the corner, one hip cocked, its head held low, and its eyes closed.

She needed to sell them. The grass was drying up in the summer sun and soon there wouldn't be anything left. No one in this area would help her find a buyer. Maybe if she could get signed in to Jeb's ancient computer, she could find an auction.

She stood and dropped her gloves to the ground. It was time for a break anyway, and while she got something to drink she could search for a livestock sale online.

The icy water tasted good after working in the summer sun, and she drank down half the glass as she did a search on Jeb's computer. There wasn't a horse sale listed nearby, and Vale, Oregon, was the closest cow sale. Did they take horses at a cow sale?

Her ex-husband, Micah, would know, but she'd promised to stay away from him and his new family. And for once in her life, she was determined to keep her promises. After sending a quick e-mail to the livestock facility asking if they sold horses, she pulled a ragged washcloth from the drawer by the sink.

It took only minutes for the water in the faucet to become icy cold. After wringing out the cloth, she wiped the sweat off her face and neck. There was a lot to be said for simple pleasures.

Weed pulling had lost its charm, not that it ever had any, and she looked around for something else to do. As she stood looking out the back window, she spied an old trailer wedged between the barn and a fence. It wasn't very big. Her truck should be able to pull it, but even if she could figure out how to hook it up, she wasn't sure how to get the animals inside. Without a doubt, she'd have to catch them first, and that meant she'd have to get near them. Getting close up to the large animals wasn't happening in her lifetime.

As she placed her glass on the counter, she noticed a piece of paper she'd found in the driveway after Bose had left the day before. When she'd broken the news about

Jeb's death, he hadn't said a word. He hadn't even looked at her, just hurried to his truck and driven away.

She turned the card over.

*Bose Kovac, Farrier.*

If she could get him to talk to her long enough, maybe she could get him to come load the horses, or maybe even take them to the sale. She thought about asking him to do it for Jeb's sake, but another thing she wasn't going to do any more was manipulate.

The worst thing he could do was to turn her down. She picked up the receiver of Jeb's black, rotary phone and dialed.

"Kovac's Shoeing."

His deep voice took her to a time when she still had possibilities. When she hadn't thrown them all away. "Bose, it's Marlene."

The line went dead.

She dialed again. "Bose, it's about the colt." Well, at least he hadn't hung up. "I need your help."

His sigh was as deep as the Grand Canyon. "Marlene, leave me alone."

Regret, hot and heavy, flashed through her nerve endings causing pinpricks of pain. Bose had been sweet and kind. He'd had loved her more deeply than anyone she'd ever met, and she'd hurt him.

"I don't know where else to turn." She talked as fast as she could before he disconnected again. "The horses are about out of grass, and there's no hay in the barn. I don't have any money to buy hay, and the only thing I can think of to do is sell them."

"What do you want from me?"

He was listening, so she kept going. "I need to sell them soon, and the closest sale is in Vale. It's a cow sale, but I think I could talk them into selling these horses. Uncle Jeb's trailer is here, and I think my truck can pull it. Could you come show me how to hook it up and load the horses for me? I won't bother you again, I promise."

The sigh he gave pushed its way through the phone line. "If only I could believe you won't be back tomorrow with another favor."

She was thankful Bose couldn't see her as her cheeks blazed in embarrassment. It would do no good to promise again. He wouldn't believe her. "You're right. This is my problem, and I'll figure out a way to take care of it. I'm sorry I bothered you." Marlene hit end before Bose could say another word. He was right. The old Marlene would have hounded him to death to get what she wanted. The old Marlene was gone.

Uncle Jeb was the only one who'd have believed her. Now, he was gone, too.

She put the receiver back into the cradle, swallowed the last of her water, and hurried out to her truck. No time like the present to see if she could figure out how to hook up the trailer.

Driving to the barn was the easy part. Trying to line up the truck and trailer proved to be a challenge. After banging the bumper of the truck into the trailer a few times, she resorted to climbing out every few inches to see how close she was. It was painstakingly slow, but she finally had the hitch and ball lined up. Impatience won out, and she decided to creep backwards until she tapped the trailer hitch. A slight bump told her she'd succeeded.

Jumping out, she hurried to the back of the truck in time to see the trailer jack roll off the block of wood and fall to the ground. No way could she get it hooked up now.

She dropped down and leaned against the tire. If she'd felt any inclination to learn what Micah had tried to teach her when they'd been married, she'd know how to do this horse stuff now.

Tires on gravel caught her attention. She peeked beneath her truck to see Bose climbing out of his.

Heaving herself to her feet, she watched as the man walked to the fence and scratched the brown horse on the neck. Marlene moved closer, being careful to stay out of reach of the animal's huge teeth. "Doesn't it scare you to be this close?" In her mind, the animal could easily jump the fence and attack them.

Bose rubbed the horse between the eyes. "This old mare wouldn't hurt anyone. She's a sweetheart, aren't you Bomber?" He stroked down her neck beneath her mane before turning toward Marlene. "You can't sell these horses through a sale. They'll go to the kill buyers."

For the first time since she'd seen Bose again, he was looking at her, but his beautiful brown eyes didn't have the warmth she remembered. They were hard and determined, and she'd made him that way.

She didn't know much about horses, but even she had heard about the controversy over whether to send horses to slaughter. People on each side of the argument had valid points, but the thought of sending Jeb's horses to their deaths made her sick. "What else can I do? I can't afford to feed them through the winter and even if I could, I'm going to fix this place up and sell it."

The colt wandered over and hung his head over the fence to claim his share of attention. The blue roan tried to crowd the old mare out of his way, but when she laid her ears back and gave him a "mare" look, he backed away.

Bose laughed. "Don't bite off more than you can chew, Louie Blues."

Marlene backed away another step. "I thought you said she was nice. She almost bit him."

Bose rubbed the mare under her chin. "She didn't have to bite him. She was just reminding him who is in charge here."

"Pardon me if I stay out of reach of those teeth. I was bitten once, and once is enough for me." Marlene rubbed a spot on her upper left arm at the memory. She stuck her hands in her back pockets, at a loss as to what to do next. Why was Bose here?

He wandered over to her truck and the trailer. Pulling

the door open, he leaned the seat forward. After digging through the mess behind the seat, he pulled out a handyman jack.

A magpie squawked from a branch overhead. When Marlene looked up, the bird cocked its head and squawked again. Nuisance birds, Jeb had called them, but she'd always thought they were pretty. Until now. This one seemed to be making fun of her.

With a few easy moves, Bose jacked up the trailer tongue and set it back on the stump. He inspected the saddle compartment before moving to the back doors. "It isn't safe to haul a horse in this old thing. You'd have to replace the floorboards."

"I don't trust horses, but I don't want them hurt. Do you have a better idea?"

He stared at the rusty trailer for so long, Marlene wondered if he'd gone to sleep. Not that she minded. With his attention on the trailer, she had a chance to study him. The man hadn't changed much in the ten years since she'd seen him. If anything, he'd gotten better looking, more rugged. She was lost in memories when he spoke.

"Possibly the second worst idea in the history of the world," he muttered. "But better than them being killed."

Marlene frowned. He'd lost her with the last statement. "I need to do something with them."

The look he gave her was filled with resignation. "The mare is well bred, and she's due to have a colt in the spring. I'll make you a deal."

She watched him, doubt causing her breath to catch. She'd never come out on top of any deal with a man. Most of the time that had been her own doing, and this was Bose. With all the hard feelings between them, she still trusted him. "What kind of deal?"

"Give the mare to me."

*~*

Before Bose could finish, Marlene cut in. "She's yours, but what about the other one?"

He shook his head. She never had been able to wait for a person to finish speaking. "I wasn't done. You give me Bomber, and let me keep her here until I get a place of my own. I'll buy enough hay to keep both of them. I'll also ride Louie Blues until we find someone to buy him."

She looked from the horses to him, her eyes wide. "You'd help me?"

Her utter disbelief caused him a moment of guilt, but then he remembered it was Marlene, and she was an expert at emotional blackmail. "I'll help the horses."

Her cheeks flushed red, and she turned her attention to the animals. "Of course. What do you need me to do?"

"You'll get more for Louie if I put some rides on him. He'll be more finished and easier to sell. That way I can make sure he goes to a good home." He fixed his attention on the horses. The old mare had been Jeb's heeling horse for the Senior Pro rodeos before arthritis made him give up the sport, and had been a favorite of Bose's. "Jeb promised me if anything ever happened to him, the mare was mine. He obviously never got around to putting it into his will." The old man always did trust his great niece more than he should have.

Bose looked at the stout blue roan. Christ! She'd been going to run them through a cow sale.

He glanced at Marlene from the corner of his eyes. She still had her attention focused on the dried-out pasture. To be honest, she hadn't known one livestock sale from another, and she had asked for his help.

He looked at her ancient truck and the even older two-horse trailer. Good thing he'd swallowed his pride and come to stop her from trying to load the horses. "What would you have done if I hadn't shown up?"

She drew in a sharp breath, straightened and turned to him.

With the breath, her breasts lifted beneath her T-shirt.

Shit! What did he have to do to get over the rush of desire he felt whenever he looked at her?

Chase it away with a dose of anger.

"Eventually, I would have gotten the trailer hooked up. That is, if I didn't kill myself in the process." She sighed as electric blue eyes found his, and a frown drew down her brows. "If I'd ended up under the trailer, how long do you think it would have taken for someone to find me? Hopefully before the horses starved to death."

Here we go. Marlene's patented sob story of how everybody was against her. He took a step toward his truck when she spoke again.

"Never mind that." She walked to the rough wooden bench beneath the Sugar Pine and sat down. Her gaze was candid and open. "If nothing else, I would have called Clinton. He wouldn't have been happy to hear from me, but he would have taken care of . . . What did you call them? Bomber and Louie Blues? He'd have made sure they didn't starve."

She leaned back against the rough bark, a rueful smile on her face. "I don't think I'll live long enough to make up for all I've done." She waved a hand. "But you don't want to hear about my problems."

She was right. Bose walked to his truck and pulled out his saddle and a blanket. "I'm going to get started on the colt." He caught the blue roan, saddled him and turned him into the pole round pen beside Jeb's barn.

Marlene followed him to the barn and stood watching as he ran the colt around to take the fresh off him. When he bridled Louie and climbed into the saddle, she moved a little closer. "Will you ride the other one, too?"

Bose took a moment to let the colt settle, enjoying the summer day. A breeze kept it from being stifling, and the smell of fresh cut hay from the neighboring place gave him a sense of peace. "She's pretty much retired as a riding horse. She'll have a colt in the spring."

A high-pitched voice surprised both of them, and they

turned to see the thin, redhead climbing through the fence. "It's a great cross, too." The girl, her hair neatly braided today, turned to Marlene. "That mare is double bred Jet Deck, and she's bred to Frenchman's Guy. What a colt this will be." Her smile lit up her face, and Bose returned her grin.

"How you doin', Wendy?" The neighbor girl had been a constant companion of Jeb's. Her dad was a long-haul trucker, and Jeb had watched her when he'd been out of town. The old man and the kid had become fast friends. She'd been intent on learning as much about horses as Jeb could teach her. His death must have hit her hard.

"Well, life ain't all cowboy boots and rodeos, but it should be." Her grin widened. "But I'm coping.

Bose recognized what had been a favorite saying of Jeb's. "I'm sorry to hear about Jeb."

She shrugged before crawling through the fence to stand by the mare, but he could see the effort she was putting into her nonchalant attitude.

Bose had listened to Jeb give the girl advice several times, and he'd been impressed.

The man was as good at reading people as he'd been with horses. Jeb had taught her patience and given her a broader outlook on life. "You want to ride Bomber?"

Wendy looked at Marlene. "Is it okay with you? I guess you own her now." The statement was matter of fact.

"Actually, Bose did some trading with me. He owns Bomber now."

The girl leapt into the air and let out a whoop. "She's yours? Man, I can't wait until the colt hits the ground. I've already got a name picked out."

He studied Marlene as she observed the girl. He'd heard she had a daughter about this girl's age, and that she didn't see her any more. He was surprised when her expression softened.

"Would you mind telling us?" Marlene leaned against the side of the barn, a smile on her face.

"I don't know. You'll think it's dumb." The outgoing girl suddenly became shy, her gaze focused on the toe of her scuffed boots.

"We won't, promise."

"Well, its daddy's name is Frenchman's Guy. Bomber's sire is Dinner Flight, and her registered name is Fine Dining." The kid turned to Marlene, giving her a lesson in naming horses. "You try to combine the two for the registration papers." She turned to Bose. "What do you think about Fine French Dining?"

If he ever had a kid, he'd want one just like Wendy. Not that having a child was going to happen. He pushed the thought away and let his grin widen. "I like the name a lot. It would work for either a filly or colt."

Wendy's smile faded, and she rolled her eyes. "No, that's a girl's name, Frenchy for short. I'm still working on one for a stud colt. What about French Cuisine? We could call him Cuss."

"We have time to think about names. It's going to be a long time before Bomber's colt arrives. Go catch your horse, and you can ride around the pasture with me."

Wendy grabbed a halter from the fence and walked toward the mare.

"I thought you said no one was riding her." Marlene's voice brought him out of his thoughts. "Isn't she pregnant?"

Wendy got the halter on the bay mare and led her up beside the fence. She scrambled onto the poles and climbed onto the horse's back.

"It isn't going to hurt her to have Wendy ride her. Besides, it keeps her in shape, and she loves that little girl." After the colt was weaned, and once he'd okayed it with her dad, he planned to give the mare to Wendy.

Marlene's voice rose. "She doesn't have a saddle."

He knew Marlene was afraid of horses, but she had been married to a rancher for several years. Surely, she'd seen someone ride without a saddle before. Without thinking, the next words jumped out of his mouth. "Doesn't your daughter ride bareback?"

The color drained from her face. In a move he hadn't seen before, she pulled her dignity around her like a blanket. "Willa Wild isn't my daughter anymore. She belongs to Micah and Cary."

STEPHANIE BERGET

# CHAPTER THREE

In the week since Bose had agreed to help her, Marlene hadn't seen him once. Loneliness wasn't a problem, though. Wendy had crawled through the fence separating their properties at least once a day and sometimes two. Marlene had worried the girl's constant visiting would be irritating, but she found she liked to see the redhead crawling through the fence separating Jeb's property from hers.

She wondered if Willa was as horse crazy as Wendy, but tried to keep her mind off her daughter. Cary was a better mother than she could ever be, and she was grateful Micah had found such a caring woman to be Willa's stepmother.

"You ever goin' to learn to ride?" Wendy squirted glass cleaner on the window over the sink and scrubbed with a newspaper. "You sure this is the best way to clean this window? My hands are turning black."

Marlene schooled her face, but she was grinning inside. The girl was worried about a little ink but didn't mind the dust and horse manure. "Yes, and your hands will wash." She swept the dust off the floor and emptied the dustpan into the garbage can beneath the sink. "I'm not ready to ride yet. How is Bose doing with Louie Blues?"

"That colt is a rascal, but he's kind and talented."

It was the girl's voice, but Marlene heard Uncle Jeb's words clear as could be. She could almost see his weathered face. He'd called Marlene his little rascal for as long as she could remember. Sadness washed over her. Uncle Jeb had been the only person who had accepted her as she was. The only one who saw her potential and hadn't felt the need to change her. The only guilt she felt was in letting him down. He'd always been sure she was destined for greatness.

"I watched you ride Bomber. How long have you been riding?" She grabbed the two small rugs in the kitchen and tossed them out the back door. "Hold that thought. I'll be back in when I've shaken these out." The one thing they weren't short on out here was dust, and it billowed up as she shook the rugs.

Wendy had moved on to the window in the dining room by the time she'd returned. "I used to come over here and watch Jeb when he worked the horses. The first time, I was only six, and my dad spanked me for running off. He said I'd scared the bejeezus out of him when he couldn't find me. Didn't stop me though." She scratched her nose and left a streak of black along the side and down her cheek. "You sure this is the best way?"

"I'm sure." Marlene spread out the rugs. Opening the refrigerator, she pulled out a can of Coke and held it up. "This is the last one. You want to split it?"

Wendy gave one last swipe to the window and dropped the newspapers in the garbage. "Sure."

"You said your dad got mad. What did your mom say?" Marlene filled two plastic glasses with ice and split the soda. She handed one to Wendy.

The girl took a long drink and set the glass on the counter. "My mom left us when I was four. Dad said she found things she liked better than us, but I think she didn't want to be a trucker's wife. Jeb told me, you gotta know what you want before you get yourself into a bad situation."

Marlene was stunned. Where had this mini adult come from? Wendy understood Marlene's life better than she did. "Have you seen your mom since?"

Wendy touched her fingertip to a droplet on the side of the glass and hurried it to the counter. "No, but Dad and I get along fine." When she looked up, Marlene couldn't see a sign of anger. "She's only doing what she has to do."

Marlene racked her brain for something wise to say, for anything to say, but her mind was blank.

Fortunately, Wendy changed the subject. "How come you're afraid of horses?" The girl swung her legs back and forth as she talked, her feet hitting the side of the island with a thump, thump, thump.

Marlene took the last swallow from her drink, dumped the remaining ice in the sink and rinsed the glass. Maybe Willa would be as forgiving as Wendy. Like the girl said, it was the only choice she could have made at the time. She stopped for a moment, and felt a smile curve across her lips. She hoped Willa Wild was as open-minded as this kid.

She forced a wider smile and turned back to the girl. "I'm not afraid. Those animals smell, so I don't get too close."

Wendy threw back her head, and her laugh bounced around the room like wind chimes in a strong breeze. "I've watched you. You're afraid."

She couldn't get anything past this kid. "You're right. When I was little, around six years old, my dad put me on a horse he was going to buy. It ran off with me. When I cried, he held me in front of it, and forced me to pet it. The damned thing bit me." Marlene shuddered at the memory. "I'm not real smart, but I do learn if it hurts enough."

Wendy hopped off the barstool and rounded the counter. She patted Marlene on the shoulder. "Horses aren't all mean. I'll help you learn to like them. We'll start with Bomber."

Marlene pulled Wendy into a quick hug then stepped back. "Thanks, but no thanks. I'm just fine staying away."

Wendy watched her for a moment before letting the subject drop. She wandered down the hallway and opened the bedroom door. Her voice rose to a shriek. "You haven't watered the plants!"

Marlene hurried down the hall and into the room. The leaves were starting to droop. She watched as Wendy raced past her with a watering can and filled it in the bathroom.

When she got back, Wendy measured the water and gave each plant a drink. The girl turned accusing eyes on Marlene. "If you're not going to take care of them, let me."

Feeling foolish for letting the girl down, Marlene fumbled for words. "I'm sorry. I forgot they were here."

"I'll take care of them from now on."

As Wendy fussed with the plants, Marlene watched. Obviously, Uncle Jeb had taught her well. "You keep calling these the plants. Do you know what they are?"

Marlene didn't know this much derision could be stuffed into such a small package. Wendy rolled her eyes. "I may be young, but I'm not stupid. Jeb grew these because marijuana helped him sleep when his arthritis bothered him. It is legal in Oregon, you know. He wasn't doing anything wrong."

"He was growing these for himself?" If so, she could pull them up and dump them when Wendy wasn't around.

"For himself and for a customer." Wendy went from plant to plant and checked on each one, murmuring nonsensical words like a mother comforting a child. "He's growing these two for a woman with cancer."

So much for throwing the plants out. She couldn't let a cancer patient down. "When will they be ready to go?" Marlene followed Wendy around the room and took her first real look at the plants. Buds were starting to form, gray-green against the bright color of the leaves.

"It's going to be a while yet."

"If you're done, let's go." Marlene ushered the kid down the hallway and out the back door. She needed to get some more groceries and with the heat ramping up, now was a good time to go. Unfortunately, she didn't have enough gas money to drive to Burns. She'd either have to risk Millie's wrath or try to talk the café into selling her some hamburger, chips and pop. She'd heard one of Cary's friends ran the café, so either option was a bad one. "I appreciate your help, Wendy, but I have some things I have to get done."

Wendy looked at her for a moment then walked away with the speed of a sloth on downers. The girl stopped at the fence and stood looking at her home across the small pasture.

Marlene knew that look. The kid would rather be anywhere but at home alone. "You want to run interference for me at the grocery store?"

Wendy whirled and was at her side in an instant, her huge smile belying her words. "If you really need me I could probably find the time."

"I need to get my purse. I'll meet you at the truck." Her Chevy still sat in front of Jeb's trailer. She hadn't gone anywhere since the first day she'd arrived. Where would she go? She didn't know one person who'd want to see her, and most would gladly run her out of town.

*~*

Bose pulled to the curb in front of Foodtown and took a minute to catch his breath. His business had kept him running non-stop for the last few days. He'd finished shoeing the Double X Ranch remuda an hour ago, and the rest of the afternoon was his.

He opened the truck door and stepped out into the heat. Hurrying across the sidewalk, he entered the grocery store and stepped into the blessed air conditioning. A young girl he didn't recognize stood behind the cash register. Millie waved then continued stocking soup in the canned goods aisle.

"Hey beautiful. How're things going?"

"Bose. Haven't seen you for a while." Millie placed the last two cans on the shelf then gave him a fierce hug like she did to everyone in town. "Did you hear about Jeb?" She straightened the last can and turned back to him. "Too bad."

"I just heard a few days ago. His niece is out there cleaning up the place." As he watched, Millie transformed from friendly town matriarch to a woman on the fight.

A bright pink flush crept up her already rouged cheeks, her hands curled into fists, and the muscle in her jaw clenched. "Why that . . ." The bell over the door rang out, cutting off her sentence. Her eyes widened then narrowed beneath her lowered brows. Someone was in trouble.

He turned to see what had set her off, and there stood Marlene and Wendy.

Millie brushed past him. "Excuse me, Bose. There's something I've got to take care of." She charged toward the front, until she stood in front of Marlene. "I thought I told you not to come in here again."

Marlene backed up a step. "I'm leaving." She touched Wendy's shoulder. "We'll go someplace else."

In all the time he'd known her, Bose had only seen Marlene back down from an argument one time, the day in high school when three football players had cornered her behind the gym. The day he'd helped her and thought they were friends.

Marlene started toward the door, but Wendy didn't. "You don't want us here?" She stood in front of Millie, her hands on her hips. "What's wrong with us?"

Millie Barnes softened her expression as she shifted her gaze to Wendy. "You're welcome here, Wendy. Anytime. Let me get you some candy." The storeowner grabbed a small white bag and scooped some jellybeans out of the bin. She held it out to the girl.

"I wouldn't eat—"

Bose cut her off. Time to step in and prevent a town scandal. Marlene might deserve Millie's scorn, but Wendy didn't.

"Wendy, why don't you go find out what groceries Marlene needs?" He placed his hand on her shoulder and moved her toward the door.

"But, Bose. Marlene's been so nice to me. This isn't fair." She struggled to make her way back to the store owner, but Bose knelt before her and waited for her to pay attention.

"Let's do this my way. You don't want Marlene's feelings to get hurt more than they are, do you?" When the girl shook her head, he pulled a five-dollar bill out of his pocket. "After you bring me the grocery list, take Marlene to the café for a Coke. I'll meet you there."

Wendy looked from him to Millie and back before nodding in agreement.

Neither adult said another word until Wendy had brought the list and disappeared back out the door.

Millie's voice was quiet when she finally spoke, but it shook with emotion. "You and Marlene?"

Bose had been watching the woman and girl cross the street to the Café, but when he heard Millie he whirled back. "What? No!"

"I watched her as she used Micah and left that little girl. Don't let her get her hooks into you." Millie picked up the bag of candy and held it out to him.

He took it. "I didn't want Wendy to become more upset. Believe me, I know all about Marlene."

"No man knows all about Marlene until she'd taken him for all he's got." Millie held out her hand. "If you're determined to get this food for her, let me help."

The list was short, only the bare necessities. He added a pound of hamburger, apples and bananas and anything he thought she'd need. Millie rang up the purchases and bagged them without a word. When she opened her mouth to speak, he held up his hand. "I appreciate your concern, but I can take care of myself."

Millie gave him a tight smile and walked to the back of the store.

Bose gathered the bags of food and put them in the bed of his truck before crossing the street to the Five and Diner Cafe.

The aroma of freshly baked pastries filled the air as he pushed open the heavy glass door to the café. He waved at a client then turned his attention to the glass display case in the center of the Five and Diner. Cary's bear claws and apple fritters were the best he'd ever tasted, and he intended to take some home with him.

The two redheads sat in a booth in the back of the café. Wendy talked a mile a minute as she scooped one spoonful of ice cream sundae after another into her mouth. Marlene's eyes studied the café as if she expected someone to burst in and throw her out the door. After the scene at the grocery, she probably did.

Bose slid onto the red vinyl bench next to Wendy. "Good?"

"Thank you, Bose. This is the best. I haven't had ice cream for ever," she said, drawing out the last word.

Marlene gave a tense laugh. "We had an ice cream sandwich yesterday."

"I know, but not this kind with all the toppings." She quieted down and concentrated on eating as if they might make her leave before she'd finished every bit.

Bose looked around the Café. He'd come in here with Jeb a few times and liked the food. The first time he'd met Pansy Lark, she'd been dressed in an I Love Lucy outfit, but since then, she'd worn jeans and a T-shirt. He'd heard she'd dressed in costumes all the time before she'd married Kade Vaughn.

After Jeb had introduced him to the bronc rider, he'd done the shoeing on the Vaughn's barrel and team roping horses.

"I'm heading back to my place. Do you want me to drop off the groceries?" Bose stood and dropped a dollar on the table for a tip. He'd noticed Marlene hadn't ordered anything.

She picked up the dollar and handed it back, replacing it with one of her own. She pushed a five-dollar bill into his hand, and with her wallet held open, she asked, "How much do I owe you for the groceries?"

There were only a few bills in the wallet. "I've got something I need to take care of. Why don't you take Wendy home, and I'll settle up with you there."

She nodded, and as Wendy put the last bite in her mouth, she smiled at the girl. "Ready to go ride?"

Marlene had a million smiles, and Bose had thought he'd seen every one. There was the one she put on when she wanted to impress a man, the one she used when she wanted to get her way, or the one she dazzled people with when she was setting up a scam. They were all blindingly beautiful, but not one held a candle to the kind, warm smile she gave to Wendy.

The girl jumped out of the booth. She gave Bose a hug. "I'm going to teach Marlene to ride Bomber."

Bose's laugh burst out before he could control it, and the look on Marlene's face widened his smile. "You might have met your match, Marly." The laughter died in his throat, and he almost choked on his own spit when his pet name for her slipped out.

Her eyes widened, and she ducked her head. "Come on, Wendy. Time to go."

As he watched them leave, the aroma of the best burgers and fries in Oregon caught his attention. He'd get the donuts for later, but for now . . . He sauntered up to the counter.

Pansy waved to him from the kitchen pass through and hurried out to take his order.

He'd grown to like this quiet woman. Kade Vaughn was a lucky man. "I'd like three Ranchhand Specials with extra fries and tater tots, to go, please."

"You got it, Bose." Pansy glanced at the back booth then looked at Bose. "Your friend leave?"

"Yeah, add whatever she ordered to mine." Leave it to Marlene to stick him with the bill.

Pansy snorted and shook her head like she'd read his mind. She strode to the kitchen door, calling out before it swung closed behind her. "She already paid. You might cut her some slack. People do change."

# CHAPTER FOUR

What had she been thinking trying to enter Millie's store again? She hadn't thought she'd had another choice. It had been stupid, she realized, to count on Millie being gone. She was going to have to spend some money on gas and drive to Burns to stock up.

To top off her day, she'd been so upset when Bose had called her Marly she hadn't insisted he tell her how much he'd spent or grabbed the groceries from his truck. She wasn't Marly any more, and wasn't sure she'd ever been the sweet girl Bose had imagined.

To waste fuel driving back into East Hope to get the food when she didn't have money to spare was foolish. Hopefully, Bose would bring it by soon. She needed to feed Wendy dinner.

Standing here looking into the bed of her truck like the food would magically appear wasn't accomplishing anything. "Hey, kiddo. How about you saddle Bomber, and I'll watch you ride. You can teach me a few things about horses."

"I'll have to teach you everything about horses. I don't think you know one single thing about them." The grin on Wendy's face softened her words.

"I know nearly as much about horses as you know about make-up."

Wendy's smile faded. "I don't know nothin'—"

Marlene cut her off. "Anything."

Wendy slumped and rolled her eyes. "I don't know anything about make-up. Daddy doesn't go in for that girly stuff, and I don't know anyone else who'd want to teach me." They'd been walking toward the barn, but Wendy stopped in her tracks and turned to Marlene. "Could you?"

The girl in front of Marlene vibrated with excitement. "If you could make me look like you, the girls wouldn't tease me."

Marlene studied Wendy. The last thing the girl needed was to be like her. She'd love to help, but she'd learned a hard lesson about overstepping boundaries. "Tell you what. You make sure it's okay with your daddy, and if he says yes, we'll have a make-up session."

"Woohoo!" Wendy danced around Marlene and performed a very unladylike bit of shadowboxing. Bomber and Louie wandered over and hung their heads over the fence to watch.

"Hold it!" Marlene kept her voice low, but put enough tone in it to get Wendy's attention.

The girl stopped in her tracks, her hands still in fists. "What?"

"There's one thing I want to make clear." Marlene leaned down until they were eye to eye. "We are not doing smoky eyes until you're twenty-one."

Wendy beamed with a too innocent expression. "Anything you say." She scampered across the barnyard, calling to Bomber. "Come on, old girl. We've got a lesson to give to my make-up artist." She brought the mare over to the barn and brushed her within an inch of her life. By the time she was done, Bomber's mane hung in silky sheet and her tail billowed in the soft breeze.

The day was unusually pleasant for mid-August in central Oregon. A light breeze filled the air with the scent of Jeb's pine tree. A covey of Quail picked their way across the mostly dead lawn and a magpie scolded her from the fence. No use watering at this late date. The new owners would have to replant in the spring.

"Bomber's ready." Wendy led the mare over from the barn. She took off the halter and showed Marlene how to put on a bridle.

"I'm not putting my hand close to her mouth."

"You will. You need some time to get used to her." Wendy adjusted the brow band and buckled the throatlatch.

Marlene spent the next half hour listening to Wendy teach her the basics of Horsemanship 101 and nodding like she understood half of what the girl said. This was what she'd imagined her life would have been like without Gran's constant interference. If she could have been a kid, a normal girl, not the next best hope for her grandmother's retirement.

Wendy's voice brought her back to the present. "Bomber wants you to pet her." The girl sat on the mare bareback and urged the horse next to the fence where Marlene stood.

Getting any closer to the big animal was the last thing Marlene wanted to do, but underneath it all, she was Gran Clegg's granddaughter. She wasn't going to have the kid call her a coward. Besides, if she could get over her irrational fear of the huge animals it would be one more item on her self-improvement list she could cross off. She might even grow to like them. Maybe.

She forced one foot and then the other closer to Bomber. Reaching out a tentative hand, she touched the mare on the tip of her nose.

The white spot between Bomber's nostrils was as soft as the cream-colored cashmere sweater she'd gotten from an admirer before she'd changed her life, and Marlene stroked the mare again.

She felt, rather than heard someone behind her. When

had Bose arrived?

"Wendy, you are a miracle worker." The dry grass crackled with each footstep as Bose crossed the lawn.

Each time she heard his voice, a shiver slid through her body. It was a useless feeling. She'd ruined her future with Bose years ago in an attempt to make her grandmother happy.

The girl puffed up with pride. "Of course, I'm a miracle worker." A frown appeared on her face. "What did I do?"

"You got Marlene to touch a horse."

His outdoorsy scent curled through her senses, and she had the urge to lean into his shoulder. She made herself take a step away and rest her elbow in the fence. Through the years, she'd become an expert at nonchalance.

Bose took the reins from Wendy and waited for the girl to slide to the ground. "If you'll get the food out of my truck, I'll put Bomber away."

He turned and smiled, and for an instant Marlene thought the look was for her. She started to grin back.

His next words squashed that thought. "Wendy, I thought you might be hungry. I brought burgers."

When was she going to learn? The smile and pleasant attitude were meant for Wendy. Just like every other person she'd met, she'd ruined any chance at having a relationship with Bose.

Getting away from East Hope, Oregon and meeting people who didn't know her background was her only option. She'd worked hard to change, but no one here was going to believe her. She didn't blame them. She'd given them all kinds of reasons not to trust her.

Wendy helped her carry the groceries into the house. Before they'd unpacked the sacks, Bose appeared in the back door with three brown paper bags.

At the scent of the burgers, and much to her embarrassment, Marlene's stomach rumbled. She hadn't eaten anything at the café. Bose had sent money with

Wendy, but taking anything from anyone in this town wasn't in her plan. She'd only had enough cash to buy Wendy the sundae.

After plopping the bags onto the counter, Bose turned to Marlene. "Sounds like you could use a burger."

She grabbed the milk and cheese and put them in the refrigerator. As she turned, Bose handed her a paper wrapped sandwich. "Don't suppose you'd have a beer in the fridge?" He sank down at the table next to Wendy and opened one of the bags.

"Not a one. I don't drink." She pulled two cokes off the six-pack Bose had bought and set them on the table. After filling a couple of glasses with ice for the soda, she set one beside Wendy's burger. She held the other one out to Bose, only to find him staring at her. She could see the doubt in his eyes.

Marlene felt heat crawl up her cheeks, and irritation flare in her chest. Just once, she'd like to make a statement without having to justify her words. "Look, I quit two years ago. If you want a beer, you'll have to bring your own or go somewhere else." She folded her arms across her chest, holding in her righteous anger.

Wendy looked from one to the other, swallowed and grinned at Bose. "You didn't even have to say a word to say the wrong thing." The kid refocused her attention to the food in front of her and ignored the tension flowing through the room.

"Sorry," Bose said, keeping his eyes on Marlene. "I remember several times when you drank everyone under the table."

He wasn't backing off a bit, and she was glad. She didn't owe him an explanation, and he did have every right not to believe her, but for once in her life, she'd decided to tell the truth no matter what. "That was in high school. Didn't you ever make mistakes when you were young?"

Bose stared at her for a moment, and she realized he'd taken her words the wrong way. "I sure did," he said, turning to stare out the window as he chewed.

She was not in the wrong here. Grabbing an orange from the bag, she shook it at him. "And what is this? I can't afford fresh fruit." She gave him her full-on Marlene glare, the one guaranteed to put the fear of god into any man.

He raised an eyebrow in disbelief.

Apparently her look intimidated every man except one.

Bose laid down his burger and finished chewing. "Wendy loves oranges. No big deal." He reached over and ruffled Wendy's hair, earning a grin from the girl.

Marlene stuffed the three oranges into a plastic grocery bag and tied the top shut. "Wendy, you take these home with you when you go." She unloaded the rest of the bags onto the counter. "What else did you buy that I can't afford?"

Wendy poked Bose in the shoulder. "You this good with all the girls? You've made her mad again without even trying."

Bose poked her back. "Geez, kid. You sound just like Jeb."

"I try." Wendy giggled and scooped her last two fries into the sauce and popped them into her mouth. She wadded up the paper and stuffed it into the bag. Stuffing her trash into the can, she turned to Marlene. "Have you watered the plants?"

Marlene backed up a step and held up her hands in mock alarm. "Not me. After the chewing out you gave me the last time, I'll leave their care up to you." The grin she'd tried to suppress broke through. "I'd like to watch you again, though. In case you can't make it over one of these days, and I have to take care of them."

Wendy grabbed a pitcher and filled it at the sink. She lugged it down the hall with Marlene following.

Marlene watched as the girl measured out precise amounts and watered each plant. She carefully checked the plugs for the grow lights.

Wendy turned to Marlene. "The buds look good. We should have Mr. Myers come over and see when they'll be ready for harvest."

Marlene had seen Mr. Myers name and number on a grubby sticky note stuck to the refrigerator. "We'll also have to find out how to harvest them."

Boot heels clicked against the fake wood floor of the hallway.

Wendy looked over her shoulder, and the smile on her face disappeared.

As Marlene started to turn, a hand roughly clasped her shoulder and whirled her around.

"What in the hell are you doing now, Marlene?"

\*~\*

Bose set her aside and strode into the room. "I can't believe you've stooped so low as to have a child help you grow marijuana." He'd thought Marlene might have changed, but even ten years after she'd screwed him over for money, he could see she was still the greedy woman who'd dumped him.

Anger and disappointment raced through his body, and he'd stopped to regain control when Wendy rushed across the room and stepped between them.

"Don't you hit her!" Fear had caused the girl's voice to go up three octaves, but she wasn't backing down. She clenched her fists and raised them to a fighting stance.

She was small, but mighty, and Bose didn't have one doubt she'd take him on if she thought she needed to protect her friend. Bose stepped back and dropped to a knee. "I'm not going to hurt Marlene."

Wendy narrowed her eyes. "How are we supposed to know you won't?"

Valid point when he thought about it. He glanced at Marlene to see her standing stock-still, her face a mask of misery. Taking a deep breath to buy some time to think, he turned back to Wendy. He needed to reassure the kid and get her away from the influence of this woman. "I'm not hitting Marlene. Is your daddy home?"

Wendy dropped her fists but not her attitude. "What does my daddy have to do with you blaming Marlene for something she didn't do?"

Marlene crossed the room and touched Wendy on the shoulder. When the girl turned toward her, she gave her a small smile. "It's not his fault, honey." She looked at Bose. Regret shone clear in her gaze. She patted Wendy once more and left the room.

Bose watched her turn into the hall and disappear from sight. He'd have given most of what he owned for things to have been different, but Marlene had ruined that idea years ago.

Wendy stared at him, not relaxing at all. "Look, kid. Adults can't have children messing around with drugs. It's not legal, and it's not healthy."

The sneer that twisted Wendy's expression would have made the snarkiest adult proud. "You're saying I would have been better off going with Child Protective Services instead of staying with Jeb after my mom left?" She wandered back to the plants and stroked the leaves with one finger. "These were his babies, you know."

Bose's thoughts had still been on Marlene when he realized he'd been wrong. He stared at the lush green plants. They were nearly three feet tall with soft gray-green buds. He'd never been up close to marijuana before. "Jeb's plants? Not Marlene's?"

An almost evil smile lit the kid's face. "Don't you listen? That's what I said. Marlene didn't even know they were here. When I showed her, she wanted to throw them out."

"That's what we should do." He stood and curled his fingers around the lip of the planter. Wendy slapped his hand. It didn't hurt, but he jerked it away in surprise.

She stood, hands on her hips like a disapproving

schoolteacher with an especially dense pupil. "These are medical marijuana plants grown for specific patients. Don't you know anything?" When he stood without answering she continued. "Patients have to go to a doctor who prescribes a particular plant then the grower grows for a specific person. If you destroy these, Jeb's client is going to have to find someone else." Her expression softened. "Don't you know anything about medicine?"

Bose shook his head. He didn't. Not this kind. He'd always thought people who used marijuana were weak or lazy. "Did Jeb use this?"

The eye roll told him he'd asked another stupid question. "He used it for his arthritis and when it became legal, he started growing to help others."

Jeb had been one of the hardest working people he'd ever known. Guess there went his lazy druggy theory. As he stood, lost in thought, he felt a small hand on his forearm.

"I think you owe Marlene an apology."

Geez, this kid sounded a lot like his mother when she was disappointed with her only son. Unfortunately, she was right. He did owe Marlene an apology.

"Okay. Come on." He followed Wendy down the hall to the kitchen. The food was still scattered across the counter. Bose looked out the kitchen window at the empty backyard. "I don't see her."

Wendy put the first of several cans of soup in the cupboard. "I'm not going to find her for you, and I'm not going to help you apologize."

She didn't look at him as she spoke, and after a minute, he hurried out the back door. As he made his way down the steps, he realized he'd kind of been hoping she'd be a buffer as he talked to Marlene. How did he get himself into this mess? All the time he'd been around Jeb there hadn't been this much drama.

The backyard and pasture were empty, so he headed for the barn. He looked into the stalls that hadn't seen an animal in twenty years and climbed the rickety ladder to scan the loft. Nothing there but bits of straw and dust in either place. As he turned to go, he heard a soft snuffle.

Between the house and the barn stood the Sugar Pine. Among the green needles and brown branches, he saw a flash of red. Marlene sat on the lowest limb, staring at the hills across the valley.

He walked to the tree and leaned against the truck, trying to force his thoughts into rational order. She swung her sneaker-clad foot in a gentle arc, and he reached out and stilled the movement.

Keeping her gaze on the horizon, she didn't acknowledge his presence.

"I owe you an apology." There, he'd said it. He heard a meadowlark sing, the buzzing of bees, and the roar of a truck's engine on the highway, but he didn't hear a response from Marlene.

She shifted her weight, glanced down the fixed her gaze on the hilltops.

"Look, Marlene. I'm sorry I jumped to the wrong conclusion." He moved around to where he could see her face and tried again. "Wendy told me I needed to apologize to you. What more do you want?"

Marlene swung down and stood in front of him. "I don't want anything. You're forgiven for jumping to the wrong conclusion. Next time try to jump to the right one, okay?"

He watched her walk toward the barn then hurried to catch up. "That's not exactly what I meant." Could he sound any more lame? "What I meant was . . ."

She whirled around, the first tear he'd ever seen her shed rolling down her cheek. "What you meant was you couldn't imagine I wasn't doing something to hurt someone. You couldn't take a moment to find out the truth. You believed I'd hurt Wendy." She stood there, her flame colored hair blowing in the breeze, looking as hurt as he'd ever seen her. "You have every right not to trust me, but all you'd have had to do was ask."

She was right. In the weeks since she'd come back, she hadn't been anything like the woman he'd known ten years ago. She'd stepped up and taken over Jeb's job of watching Wendy when her dad was out of town. She'd let Millie's tirade go without a battle. She'd even gotten close to the horse to make Wendy happy. The old Marlene wouldn't have done any of that.

"You're right. You're right about all of it." He reached out and wiped the bit of moisture off her cheek, hoping this apology would hit the mark. "I'm sorry I misjudged you, and I'll try not to do misjudge you again."

STEPHANIE BERGET

# CHAPTER FIVE

For the thousandth time in the week since Bose had apologized, Marlene relived his words. Not that she believed them. After what she'd done, he'd never trust her again, but his attempt warmed her through and through. And maybe someday, he'd realize she'd been young and had listened to bad advice.

She blew an escaped lock of hair out of her eyes and stepped back from the wall to examine her work. She'd never painted anything except her nails before, but the dining room wall looked better than it had when she'd started. That was a win in her book.

This place was changing from an old bachelor's pad to a clean, bright home. It would never be new again, but with Wendy's help, it was improving. A part of her wished she could stay, but she couldn't.

With a suddenness that took her breath away, Jerry's face flashed before her eyes. She carefully propped the paintbrush on top of the can and sank to the floor.

She'd kept her friend out of her thoughts by sheer will power for almost two years. Leave it to Jerry to decide she'd waited long enough. His voice whispered in her head. "Go for your dreams, kitten."

Her smile was tinged with sadness for a friend lost too soon. "Okay, okay. I'm working on getting my life back. Don't push me."

The first time she'd met him, his musical voice had soared through the bar where his band played. He'd just finished his rendition of Johnny Cash's *Walk The Line* when he'd knelt down on the stage and looked at her.

"Of all the gin joints in all the towns in all the world, she walks into mine."

Marlene hadn't known what he'd meant, and from that day until the day he'd died, he'd teased her about her lack of knowledge of old movies. A sigh rocked her body, and once again, she regretted that the truly good people seemed to go first.

Crawling to her feet, she put memories of Jerry back into the special place in her mind where she kept them, grabbed the paintbrush and headed for the sink. There'd been enough painting and more than enough reminiscing for one day.

As she washed the brush, she saw Bose pull into the lot. He and Jerry couldn't have been more different if she'd set out to have one at each end of the spectrum, except for one attribute. Each was kind and accepting.

Jerry had been a thin wiry man who'd loved music and his cat, and was a night owl. Bose had muscles most men envied, was a dog person, and was up at dawn most days. She patted the brush dry as she watched Bose head to the barn.

She'd watched him ride the colt at least three times a week, and the animal seemed to her to be gentling down quickly. Actually, she hadn't noticed the difference until Wendy had pointed it out to her.

She slid the door shut behind her and wandered across what used to be a lawn. Uncle Jeb must have been sick for longer than anyone knew because his home, including his yard, were points of pride with him. He'd never have left it to dry out if he could have helped it. She'd have to ask

Wendy. The kid seemed to know everything.

Bose gave her a lop-sided grin as he led the colt out of the barn. It might be her imagination, but his smiles didn't look as forced as when he'd first arrived. "I'd like to watch you ride, but if you'd rather I left, I can leave."

He finished bridling the colt before he looked up.

"Never mind. I know some people don't like . . ."

"Marlene. Quit apologizing. You don't have to tiptoe around me."

His brown-eyed stare set her nerves to tingling. Don't let me be attracted to Bose. A friend was all she could hope for and friendship was pushing things. "Can I ask a few questions?"

He looked surprised. "Sure, if I have the right to refuse to answer."

"Deal." She moved closer and stroked her hand down the colt's neck. Wendy's persistent lessons were working. She wasn't terrified being this close to the horse. "Jeb has some bits hanging on the wall, but they don't look anything like this one."

"Those are handcrafted silver bits made for a horse that knows a lot more than this one. One is a Garcia from the forties. They're worth a lot. When you get ready to sell them, ask me about pricing." He flipped the reins over the animal's head. "I'd like a chance to buy a couple before you let everyone else have a look."

"Sure," she said as he swung a leg over the roan. "Come in any time and pick out the ones you want. Can you find a value on them for me?"

"I'll do that. You can sit on the fence and watch me ride if you want."

Marlene spent the next forty minutes watching Bose work the colt. Muscles rippled beneath the fabric of his shirt, and he took his time with the roan. When she asked questions, he explained what he was doing in simple enough terms even she could understand.

When he stepped down, she jumped off the fence.

"Wendy's dad sent over some pork, and I didn't know what to do with it, so I looked up a recipe in one of Uncle Jeb's cookbooks. I'm making crockpot Carnitas. I don't know if it will be edible or not, but do you want to have dinner with me? I mean not with me, but with Wendy and me. It's not like I'm asking—"

"Take a breath, Marlene. You must be in a contest to see who can talk the longest without taking a breath." His chuckle helped her relax. "I'd like to have dinner with you and Wendy."

This being nice to everyone was exhausting. Before, she'd always been figuring an angle and hadn't had time to get nervous. "Wendy's dad is leaving in about an hour, and she'll be over. Come on in when you're ready." She started for the house then turned back to Bose. "And Bose, thanks."

His brows drew together in confusion. "For what."

She'd been about to say for not hating her, but that sounded needy as all get out. "For treating me like a normal person and not a pariah."

"To be honest, I'm still not one hundred percent sure of you, but you've been acting like a normal person since you've been back, so why not?" He turned and disappeared into the barn.

He still didn't trust her, but she couldn't blame him. That he'd given her the benefit of the doubt made her smile, and she hurried to check on the Carnitas.

The sound of voices caught her attention as Bose and Wendy appeared in the doorway. "I'm starved," Wendy called to her. "But I'm going to check on the plants before we eat, okay?" Before Marlene could say anything, Wendy disappeared down the hallway.

She looked a Bose. "Want a beer?"

"I thought you didn't have money for frills."

"I found a ten dollar bill beneath the sofa when I was vacuuming and decided to splurge." She pulled a cold Keystone from the fridge and handed it to him. "I hope this kind is okay. It was on sale."

His face twisted in distaste, and he didn't take the beer from her hand. "I don't know, Marlene. I'm pretty high class. Don't know if I can drink sale beer."

She figured out he was joking about the same time as his face broke into a smile. He took the can and popped the top. "This is the brand I usually drink."

At the sound of Wendy's footsteps racing down the hall, Marlene pulled off the top off the crockpot. She'd already set out the tortillas, cheese, lettuce and tomatoes. She handed the bottle of salsa to Bose to open and pulled plates from the cupboards. "You guys might want to take a small portion at first. I'm not much of a cook."

She tried to smile as if she was cracking a joke, but she hadn't cooked much and was worried about what Bose would say. "At least I bought Rodriguez Tortillas. If all else fails, we can melt cheese on them and not go hungry."

The cookies she'd baked for Wendy's lunches were still on the cooling racks, and she busied herself arranging them on a plate while Bose and Wendy dished up their dinner. At least she knew the cookies were edible. She kept her back to the table so she couldn't see their grimaces if they didn't like the pork.

The silence drew out until she had to look. Both Bose and Wendy were eating like they were starving.

"Are they okay?" She couldn't quite keep the pleading tone out of her voice.

Wendy and Bose both nodded and kept eating. At least they weren't throwing it into the garbage or gagging. Marlene scooped a bit onto a tortilla and took a bite. It was okay. No, better than okay. It was good.

Bose stood and walked over to her. He bumped her shoulder with his, moving her over a few inches. "Trying to hog the good stuff?" He scooped another large spoonful onto a tortilla. "You've got a hit here, Marlene."

*~*

Bose turned off the key and stepped out of the truck, taking a moment to stretch out his knotted back muscles. Isaac Joyce's mare was always a pain in the ass to shoe, but he couldn't find it in him to turn the old man down when he called. Isaac had been Jeb's oldest friend and a good cowboy in his own right. The only reason the sorrel mare didn't stand like a rock was because Isaac's heart problems kept him from schooling the horse.

So, while he wrestled with the mare, Bose smiled and acted like she was a sweetheart.

He took a moment to stretch his neck, trying to work out the kinks in his shoulders and arms. He loved shoeing, but the physical wear and tear was tough.

As he started toward the barn, he heard the back door shut. Marlene jumped down the steps and hurried over to him. "Are you going to ride?"

"Gotta catch the little bugger first." He looked to the far end of the pasture to where the two horses stood near the creek, grazing on the little bit of remaining grass.

He whistled and both horse's heads came up. Bomber ambled toward them, her head swinging with her gait. Louie came half way before stopping and trotting back to the creek". Guess he's decided he doesn't want to be caught today."

"What are you going to do?" Marlene reached over the fence and scratched Bomber behind the ear. She leaned farther in and ran her hand down the mare's neck.

Bose watched her out of the corner of his eye. Wendy's lessons were working miracles. When he'd known Marlene years ago, she wouldn't have come within twenty feet of a horse. He grabbed the bucket of grain and ducked between the peeled pine rails. "Come with me, and I'll show you."

She stiffened, and her eyes grew wide. She started to shake her head then stopped. With a short nod, she slid through the fence and stood close to him. "I'll take your word it's safe."

"That's new," he said as he started across the field, Marlene glued to his side. "The only person you ever really trusted was your Gran."

She stopped, and he waited for her to speak, to defend the woman whose advice she'd taken to heart to the detriment of everyone else. Wondering what excuse she'd come up with this time, Bose braced himself for the inevitable jolt of disappointment.

"It took me a long time and a lot of heartbreak to realize Gran wasn't right about much of anything." She maintained eye contact for a short second then looked away. With a short gasp, she stepped behind Bose. "Look, he's running at us."

Bose tore his gaze away from her beautiful face to see Louie trotting across the pasture. "He's a greedy little bastard. He can't resist the thought of grain." The blue colt stuck his head in the bucket. Bose set it on the ground and worked a rope halter onto the horse's head. He scooped a handful of grain out and fed it to Bomber. "Give Bomber another bite. This guy's had enough."

Marlene picked up the bucket as Bose made Louie step back. Bomber took a couple of delicate bites then licked the bucket clean. "That one," Marlene said as she pointed at the colt. "He still scares me, but I love Bomber."

"I never thought I'd see the day."

"Horses are another thing Gran was wrong about—one of the least important." Marlene kept her distance from Louie as they walked back to the barn, but gave Bomber one last pat before climbing through the fence. "When you're finished with him, come on in. Dinner is about done."

Bose finished up and headed for the house as Wendy got off the school bus. They walked in together. Wendy dumped her backpack onto the table and danced across the room to Marlene. "Guess what?"

Marlene's face lit up when she smiled at the girl. "You

got all As?"

"No, of course not. Guess again." Wendy grabbed a glass out of the cupboard. She filled it with water, but set it onto the counter without taking a drink. "Make it a good guess."

Marlene took her time thinking then lifted her shoulders. "I don't know. Why don't you just tell me?" She pulled Wendy into a hug then laughed as Wendy wiggled her way free.

"They're having a Halloween dance, and Robby Lynn asked if I was going to be there. He's so cute, and this is the first time he's talked to me. I can go, can't I?"

Marlene's smile froze, and her gaze shifted to Bose.

"Is this a school dance?" Bose thought back, and he couldn't remember going to a dance when he was as young as Wendy, but then he'd been more interested in horses and football. The only girl he'd ever been drawn to had been Marlene, and look how that had turned out.

"You know my daddy won't let me date. It's a town dance. All the kids and adults will be there." She turned to Marlene. "You'll take me, won't you?"

Bose knew Marlene would do nearly anything Wendy asked, but he also knew what kind of reception she'd get.

"Maybe next year, sweetie." Marlene's shoulders drooped in defeat. "I can't right now."

Wendy gave Marlene a one-armed hug and a half-hearted smile. "It's okay. I didn't want to go anyway. I just didn't want to disappoint Robby."

"Why can't you go?" Bose leaned against the counter as he watched Marlene. "I think as long as we got Wendy home by ten her father wouldn't mind."

Marlene's head snapped up, and she stared at him. He could see the suspicion in her eyes. "Wendy, could you water the plants?"

"I watered them yesterday." Wendy's pale red brows drew down in confusion.

"Then could you go make sure they aren't over-watered?" Marlene looked at the girl. "Please."

When Wendy left the room, Marlene turned her blazing blue gaze on him. "What is going on here? Do you want Wendy to see the good people of East Hope pick me to pieces?" She huffed out a breath and paced from one end of the kitchen to the other. "I though we'd become if not friends, at least friendly acquaintances. I'm sorry for what I did to you. You'll never know how sorry I am for running out on you without a word. I'm sorry for every horrible thing I did to everyone, and I'm trying to make up for it. I know Micah's friends will never forgive me, but I'd hoped you would give me a chance to prove I've changed."

She dropped to a chair and buried her head in her arms. Wendy had come back down the hall and stood watching them. Her soft words barely made it to his ears. "Don't yell at her."

Bose walked to Wendy and laid a hand on her shoulder. "I'm not mad at Marlene, but I do need to clear some things up. Could you please leave us alone for a few minutes? Then I'll answer your questions."

Wendy nodded, patted Marlene on the shoulder and went outside.

Bose waited until the girl had closed the door then he sat across the table from Marlene. "You really think I'd do that to you?"

She raised her head, her cheeks flushed. "Why not? I screwed you over. Now is a great time to get back at me." The oven timer went off with a loud buzz, startling them both. Marlene jumped up and pulled a large roasting pan out of the oven. She set it on a rack and turned back to him.

"Yes, you did." He stood and moved closer. "And for a long time, I hated you."

"You have every right."

"But hate doesn't get a person anywhere, and I think you have changed." The disbelief in her eyes saddened him. In her world, no one forgave anyone for anything.

He'd discovered, not too long ago, that hanging onto anger hadn't hurt anyone but him. "I just want to take you and Wendy to the dance."

"If you are seen there with me, this town will hate you, too."

"Let 'em."

# CHAPTER SIX

Wendy stood by the pasture fence and watched Bose and Marlene talking in the kitchen. He didn't seem to be yelling. After what seemed like forever, Bose came out the door and walked over to her.

She was afraid to ask, but was more afraid of not knowing. "Is Marlene leaving?"

Bose sat on a stump next to the fence and picked up a dry blade of grass. He ran it thought his fingers then looked at her. "What would make you think she was leaving?"

Wendy rolled another piece of firewood closer to Bose and sat it on end. She plunked down and got her own piece of grass, mimicking his movements. "The only time I heard my daddy yell was right before my mama left. If Marlene gets mad at you, she'll leave. I don't want to go to the dance if it will make her leave." She'd tried as hard as she could to keep the tears back, but her voice hitched, and she had a hard time getting all the words out.

Bose looked bleary as she studied him through her tears. He'd been Mr. Jeb's friend, and he was her friend. His kind brown eyes and his smile always made her feel safe. When he pulled her onto his lap, she laid her head on his shoulder.

"Marlene isn't going to leave because you asked to go to a dance or because I said something she didn't like. She's tougher than that."

"Then why is she upset?" Wendy had never seen Marlene upset about much of anything except . . . "It's the woman from the grocery store, isn't it?" Millie had always been nice to her, but she'd yelled at Marlene the only time they'd been in Foodtown.

He was silent for a while. "There are people in town who don't like Marlene because of some things she did a while ago. They haven't had time to get over their anger."

"Like Miss Millie?" Wendy was having a hard time reconciling the friendly woman she'd grown to know with the angry woman she'd seen in the store with Marlene.

"Yes, like Miss Millie."

Marlene's voice startled Wendy, and she looked up to see her friend standing not far away. "I did some bad things and hurt people here. They haven't forgiven me."

"I don't need to go to the dance. We do fine out here by ourselves." She pasted what she hoped was a happy smile on her face and grinned at Marlene through her tears.

Bose stood her on her feet, took her hand, and looked into her eyes. "I think it's time this town got over their anger." He turned to Marlene. "Wendy and I are going to the dance. We'd like you to come with us." He held his hand out to Marlene.

Wendy held out her hand, too. She didn't care what the townspeople or God himself thought about Marlene. Wendy loved her.

*~*

Marlene's insides crawled with dread, and she poured out the glass of milk she'd gotten to settle her stomach. Nothing was going to make this easier.

In twenty minutes, Bose would be here to pick up them for the dance. Wendy had been vibrating with excitement all day, and it had been all Marlene could do to keep her misgivings hidden.

"He's here! He's here!" Wendy came running out of her bedroom and threw open the back door.

Damn! He was early, and she hadn't applied her make-up. Not that it would make any difference. Even if she looked her best, all of Micah's friends would hate her. And everyone in East Hope was a friend of her ex-husband's.

Bose stuck his head in the door. "Ready?"

She stood dumbstruck at the thought of getting in the truck and actually going to face all of her enemies. She was still frozen to the spot when Bose smiled as if he could read her thoughts. She'd be damned if she looked like a coward in front of him, so she gave him a wobbly smile. "We're ready." She reached for Wendy's hand but was a split-second too late.

The girl let out a loud whoop and raced out the door toward the truck.

Bose's grin widened. "I see you've been giving her lessons in acting like a lady."

"Like I know how to do that." Marlene felt some of the tension that had been her constant companion since Wendy had first mentioned the dance fade away. "Acting like a lady never got me anywhere."

Bose's eyes twinkled. "I'd have to argue with you."

Before she could question him on what he'd meant, Bose was striding toward the truck, too. He looked over his shoulder. "You coming?"

Marlene picked up the faux Pendleton wool poncho she'd left draped over the chair and followed them out the door. She'd spent hours trying on clothes, trying to find the perfect outfit only to realize it didn't make a bit of difference how she dressed. She left the cute, sundress hanging in the closet, and the shirt, leggings, and knee boots spread across the bed, and opted for a pair of jeans, a white T-shirt and a pair of worn cowboy boots. No use giving the good people of East Hope any more ammunition.

She caught Bose's attention before they joined Wendy in the truck. "Be sure to compliment Wendy on her makeup." When he gave her a questioning look, she smiled. "I spent almost two hours this afternoon applying lip gloss and eye shadow. It's hard when you want it to look like she isn't wearing any."

Bose grinned and climbed behind the wheel. He turned to the girl and put his fingers on her chin, turning her face one way then the other. "What's different about you? You look older or something."

Wendy pushed his hand away, but she couldn't keep the pleasure out of her voice. "I don't know what you're talking about. I'm the same old me." When she turned to Marlene, she was grinning like the Cheshire cat.

The two hours spent making Wendy happy had been worth every minute.

It was a few minutes after seven by the time they arrived. Bose found the last open space in the Grange parking lot, turned off the key and swiveled to face the girls. "Who gets the first dance?"

Marlene took a deep breath. She clasped her hands together to keep them from shaking. There wasn't any way out now.

Wendy poked her gently in the shoulder then a little more forcefully, in an attempt to get her out of the truck.

"I'm going." Marlene pushed the door open and stepped out. If she hadn't made a move, she suspected Wendy would have crawled across her lap in an attempt to find Robby. She stepped out, and pulled her poncho tight against the chill.

The girl scrambled out behind her. Her grin widened. "I didn't want to miss the whole dance while you sat here deciding whether to go in or not."

Marlene looked down at this wonder child who had

become such a big part of her life. What was she going to do when Jeb's place was sold? Her thoughts must have become clear because Wendy's smile dropped away.

Marlene put her arm around the girl's shoulder and started toward the door. "What are you waiting for? If you keep dilly-dallying, the cookies will be all gone."

Golden light from inside the hall welcomed them, and the local country band had the dance floor full. The oldest and the very youngest sat in chairs along the walls and pretty much everyone else danced, chatted or helped themselves to the array of goodies.

Bose put his hand on the small of her back and urged her inside. As they walked along the edge of the room, voices fell silent. Soon every eye was on Marlene, many of them glaring. Even the band stopped playing.

If only a hole would open up in the floor and swallow her.

Bose leaned close and whispered in her ear. "Can I have this dance?"

She whirled toward him, her panic clawing at her insides, trying to burst free. "I think I should leave. I'll walk home. You bring Wendy." She'd started for the door when he caught her hand.

"Don't let them see you sweat." His grip on her hand steadied her. He was right.

She had every bit as much right to be here as anyone else. She let him lead her to the dance floor.

Bose said something to the band, and they struck up *I Cross My Heart* by George Strait. One of her favorite songs. Bose pulled her into his arms, and for a few moments she forgot they were the only ones on the dance floor. His scent surrounded her, pulling her into the safety and peace of his world.

As the song trailed off, Bose took her hand and pulled her toward the refreshment table. He smiled and joked with the church ladies serving the sweets and punch while she tried for invisibility.

Marlene kept her gaze on the chocolate cookie in the napkin Bose had handed to her. With every eye in the place on her, there was no way could she swallow even a bite of it.

Bose led her to an empty space near the wall. "Keep your eyes on me."

"What?" His smile helped chase away the tension gripping her stomach.

"Marlene, Bose." Wendy raced across the floor. A blond boy at least an inch shorter than her followed behind. "This is Robby Lynn." She stood back and smiled as if she'd won first prize in the friend contest.

Bose stuck out his hand and the boy shook it tentatively. "Lynn? Is your dad Mason Lynn?"

"Yes, sir." The boy blushed to his roots, rocking from heel to toe, unable to stand still.

"I've been out to your place. I shoe horses for your dad."

"Yes, sir. You shoe my horse, Bandit." Talking horses seemed to relax the kid. He quit twisting his fingers, and his face faded to a normal color.

After a few minutes of watching her friend talk about shoeing with Bose, Wendy took his hand. "We're going to find the other kids." She waited until Marlene gave her permission before racing away.

Marlene turned to find Bose talking to an old rancher from south of town and began to relax. Sure, the townspeople stared at her, and not one person had smiled, but the dance hadn't been as bad as she'd feared. After all, no one had yelled or called her names.

Reaching out, she touched her fingertips to the back of Bose's belt. If she was going to do this, the strength his presence provided was essential. She straightened her shoulders and pulled her courage into a tight knit ball. She could do this. It might even be fun.

As she raised her gaze to look around the room, the blood drained from her brain.

Cary West strode toward her.

Marlene had treated Micah's new wife like a scullery maid in the short time before she'd left the area. The woman had every right to dislike her, they all did. The hot blush of shame crawled through her. She whirled, trying to find a way to escape, but she was surrounded. A hand touched her shoulder.

"Marlene. We heard you were in town." Cary's pale hair glowed in the lights.

Marlene was pretty sure everyone in town had heard she was back by this time. She raised her gaze to meet Cary's. There didn't seem to be animosity in the woman's expression, just curiosity, but Marlene wasn't letting down her guard. "I'm cleaning up my uncle's place, getting it ready to sell."

The music seemed to fade away along with the sound of people talking. Were they all listening again?

Cary's expression was noncommittal. "Willa is here."

The words hit like a shot to her chest. Of course she'd known her daughter might be at the dance, but Micah hated big gatherings and only went to a few. "I can leave. I don't want to upset her." She looked over Cary's shoulder to see her ex-husband striding across the room. The look on his face wasn't as accepting as his wife's.

Before he could say anything, Cary laid her hand on his arm. "Micah, remember what we talked about." His countenance softened when he looked at Cary, and hardened again as he raised his gaze to Marlene. "We decided if we kept the fact that you're in town from Willa and she found out later, she'd be upset. I don't want her upset, but there's not much I can do about that with you back in the area, is there?"

The urge to take a step back was strong, but Marlene stood her ground. "I'll be gone soon, Micah."

"Not soon enough. Cary's going to tell her you're here. It will be her decision whether to talk to you or not." He took his wife's hand and turned to go.

Marlene felt a warm presence at her back. "Micah. Cary." Bose stuck out his hand to the couple.

Micah hesitated before grasping Bose's hand. "I'm surprised to see you with Marlene. You don't learn very quick, do you?"

Cary turned her husband away and gave him a little push. "I don't think this is the place for a reunion. If Willa decides she wants to see you, I'll be in touch." She followed her husband, and they disappeared into the crowd.

Every eye was on Marlene. She faded back behind Bose, and turned her attention to the dust ball in the corner of the large room. Thank goodness Cary had offered to set up a meeting if Willa wanted to see her mother. Having a reunion with her daughter in front of the town was the stuff of Marlene's nightmares.

Bose put his arm around her shoulder and led her onto the dance floor. By the time she'd stumbled through another number, she'd regained some semblance of composure. As they stood in the center of the room, she caught sight of her daughter working her way between the couples. Wild red curls danced out of control around her head.

"Willa."

# CHAPTER SEVEN

Bose was talking to a client when he saw Marlene dash toward the door. She was out and gone before he could catch her. He looked around but didn't see anything amiss. Sure, the people of East Hope hadn't been exactly welcoming, but no one except her ex-husband had been overtly rude.

He said a quick good-bye and hurried out the door.

Wendy stood a few feet from the entrance, staring into the parking lot. The girl hurried over to him. "What happened? Marlene just ran by."

Bose put his hand on her shoulder. "I don't know. You wait here, and I'll find her." Wendy pointed, and Bose took off through the cars and pickups. He searched the whole area, but there wasn't a sign of Marlene.

When he got back to the Grange, Wendy and her father were waiting.

"I didn't know you were going to be at the dance, Gerald."

"Took some doing, but Wendy wanted me here." The man grinned down at his daughter, and gave her a quick hug.

"Didn't you find Marlene?" Wendy tugged at Bose's

shirtsleeve, pulling him back to the more important issue. "Where is she?"

The music filtered out to the parking lot as Bose looked around again. "I don't know." He turned to Wendy. "I'm sure you want to dance with your dad. Don't worry, I'll find Marlene."

"Don't you need our help?" Wendy's small worry-lined face stared at him.

This kid was someone special. Gerald was a lucky man. "Look, you go enjoy your dance. Marlene will be just fine. She probably got too warm and needed some fresh air." Bose started to walk away when he heard Wendy.

"I'm a kid, but I'm not stupid you know."

He turned back and gave her a tight smile. "You're right. I'm worried too, but I'll find her. Do you trust me?"

Wendy wrapped her arms around her waist. Her whispered voice was barely audible. "Yes."

"Then go introduce your father to Robby." Bose waited until Wendy and her father were back inside before making another round of the parking lot. There was still no sign of Marlene, so he started his truck and began driving the roads around town. He came upon her about half way out to Jeb's trailer.

Bose pulled up beside her and rolled down the window. "Need a ride?"

She kept walking.

"It's at least two more miles home. Climb in. I won't ask questions."

Marlene stopped walking, but she continued to stare down the road. With a sigh, she opened the door and crawled into the cab.

When they pulled into Jeb's driveway, Bose parked in front of the house, and turned off the truck. Silence filled the cab. He wondered what had set Marlene off, but he'd promised not to ask.

When she turned to him, her face was pulled into a frown. "I don't know what to do. The dance was not the place to talk to Willa for the first time in three years, but Micah would furious if I go to the ranch. I can't leave until I sell this place, but . . ." She dropped her head back onto the seat and closed her eyes.

"Did you see Willa? Is she why you left?" Bose twisted in his seat until he faced her. The desire to reach out and touch her was strong, but he kept his hands by his sides.

"Yes!"

"Why didn't you just talk to her?"

She rolled her head far enough for him to see her eyes. "What if she'd said she hated me? In front of everyone. I try not to care what the townspeople think, but I don't want to embarrass my daughter any more than I already have."

Bose reached across the cab and pushed a stray lock of hair behind her ear. "What if she just wanted to talk to her mama?"

Marlene climbed out of the truck and walked to the back yard. Louie came to the fence and hung his head over for some loving. She reached out without hesitation and rubbed the gelding between the eyes. "I can't seem to do anything right." She dropped her forehead to the top rail and wrapped her arms over her head.

Bose put his arms around her and pulled her close. "We can all only do the best we can. It isn't always right, but if you're doing your best, it's enough." He moved back far enough to turn her until she faced him. Leaning down, he gave her a soft kiss. In all these years, her scent hadn't changed. He breathed in deep. No way would he get serious about Marlene again. Another broken heart wasn't in his future, but he would be her friend.

When their lips touched again, she froze. Drawing back, she looked into his eyes. "You don't want to get mixed up with me. All I do is hurt people."

He shook his head. Maybe in the past that had been true, but she was making a massive effort to change the way she lived her life. "You haven't hurt Wendy or me."

"But, I will when I leave." She put her hands on his waist. "And, I have to leave. You know that."

"Wendy is a smart kid. She'll understand, and I'll miss my friend, but I won't be hurt. I'm not in love with you."

She tilted her head as she thought about what he'd said. "So, we're friends?"

"As far as I'm concerned we are." He pulled her into a hug and kept her close. "Good friends." Bose took her hand and led her toward the house. He stepped back and allowed her to enter first.

Marlene stopped when they got to the living room. "How good of friends are we?"

He'd been fighting his attraction to Marlene from the moment he saw her running for help. What was it with this woman? He'd felt this same pull when he'd first seen her their junior year of high school.

He took her into his arms. "Just to be clear. This is a short-term thing, until you leave or we decide to call it off."

She touched his cheek and traced her fingertip down to his collarbone. "Short term? I can do short-term, but you need to be sure."

"Marlene, I'm a big boy. I'm not in love with you, and I'm not looking for any kind of relationship with anyone. If it works for you . . ."

She reached up and touched his cheek.

The tingle that went clear to his toes was a purely physical reaction. He didn't do emotional anymore. Their kiss went from sweet to hot in the time it took for a celebrity to get a divorce. He lifted and Marlene wrapped her legs around his waist.

Without another thought about the past or the future, he got lost in the heat. "The couch is right here, but I'd much rather use a bed." When Marlene pointed down the hall, Bose carried her to the open bedroom door.

A cheap, tan bedspread covered the bed and one window was covered with a faded towel, but Marlene's citrusy scent filled the room and a flowery pillow gave it a feminine touch.

Her legs slid to the floor, and she took a step back. Staring into his eyes, she pulled the T-shirt over her head and let it drop.

Years ago, she wouldn't have been caught dead in a white cotton bra, but looking at her now, Bose hadn't seen anything sexier. He ran his hands from her waist to the sides of her breasts and slid his thumbs beneath the edge of her bra.

He felt her chest expand as she sucked in a breath. He'd dreamed about these breasts for years.

"My turn." She reached up and kissed his lips before tugging his shirt out of his Wranglers and working it over his head.

The light scratch of her fingernails made his heart race, and he pulled her into another kiss.

As much as he hated to admit it, no other woman had ever set him on fire like this redhead. If only he could trust her. Trust. The word acted like a bucket of cold water, and he dropped his hands and took a step away. What the hell was he thinking? He was acting like he had ten years ago, throwing caution to the wind, thinking with the wrong head.

Marlene tilted her head. She reached for her T-shirt and held it in front of her body. "I knew this wasn't a good idea. You're not ready, and I'm not sure I am either."

Did she think he couldn't control his emotions? Maybe he couldn't, but he knew it was time to throw caution to the wind and take what he wanted. Just as long as there were not strings attached.

With a smile, he tossed away the T-shirt before reaching around and unhooking her bra. When it fell to the floor, he found heaven for the first time in ten years.

The slight squeak of the front door opening then light footsteps in the hallway burrowed into his consciousness. He barely had time to brace his foot against the bedroom door before a knock sounded.

Wendy's voice called out. "Marlene, are you alright?"

Marlene tried to jump away, but Bose held her close. She buried her face in his chest until she had control of her giggles. "Yes, honey. I'm fine. Is your daddy here?"

"No. He drove all the way from Burns to dance with me, but he had to get back on the road."

"Well, that's too bad." Marlene stepped back, her hand fanning her face. "I'll be out in a minute. Why don't you make us some hot chocolate?"

"Kay." There was a slight pause. "You're sure you're okay?"

"I'm fine."

The light footsteps faded as Wendy moved toward the kitchen.

Bose pulled Marlene tight against his body and sighed. He'd forgotten the heaven of her soft skin against his. If only Wendy had shown up an hour later. He bent and picked up Marlene's bra and shirt. "I was supposed to call her."

Marlene tilted her head and grinned up at him. "She probably saved us from a terrible mistake."

Bose kissed her on the forehead then grabbed for his shirt. "Or a memorable time."

\*~\*

Another shiver raced down Marlene's back, and she leaned against the dusty gardening shed wall. It had been a week since Bose had brought her home from the dance, and every day her thoughts had bounced back and forth between worrying about Willa and craving Bose's touch. Each kept her in a state of confusion for differing reasons.

It would be so easy to fall for Bose. Ten years had passed, and she now realized she'd never gotten over him. Through the years, when she'd wanted to really punish herself, she'd imagined what her life would have been like if she'd ignored Gran's advice and stayed with him.

Her grandmother's words echoed through the shed like the woman was standing before her. "Your good looks only last a little while, girl. Use 'em or lose 'em. I'm counting on you."

Even though her grandmother had reminded her daily to marry for money, Marlene had made up her mind to accept Bose's proposal. They'd get by somehow. Love was more important than money, after all.

It had been a decade, but the memory was as clear as if it were happening today. Gran spent over a week trying to convince Marlene marrying Bose was the wrong thing to do, but in the end, grudgingly gave her blessing.

Two days later, she'd sat with her grandmother, waiting for a follow-up doctor's appointment, making a list of what she'd need for the wedding. She didn't need much. It would be simple, only her grandmother, Uncle Jeb, and Bose's parents. Maybe they'd take a couple of days and go to Reno for a honeymoon.

Those plans disappeared with the doctor's first words. Advanced kidney cancer. Without insurance, the cost of treatment was unmanageable.

In a panic, she'd found the first man who she'd thought had money and convinced him she was the love of his life.

Micah had even agreed to have Gran move onto the ranch.

Her grandmother fought them with every withered muscle in her body over the move. For some reason, she wanted to stay in her small, rundown home even though she'd pushed Marlene to marry up. Micah had helped her clean out the ranch's master bedroom so Gran could have her privacy, but the morning of the move, her grandmother had had a stroke. She'd lingered for six days in the hospital before giving in to death.

Out of habit, Marlene raised her hands to push her hair behind her ears. It took a moment to remember she had no long curls left. This morning, in a spur of the moment decision, she'd taken the scissors and cut her hair pixie short. It was a little uneven, but her waves hid most of the mistakes.

Sheer vanity had prevented her from ever cutting her hair before. But, if she was serious about changing her life, her appearance was a good place to start. Besides, getting rid of her long hair cut twenty minutes off her morning schedule, and she kind of liked the feeling of freedom.

Marlene grabbed the shovel and leaned it against the outside of the shed. She'd loved Gran more than anyone except Bose, Uncle Jeb and possibly Jerry, but her advice had been crap.

Dwelling on one of the more painful times in her life wasn't getting her anywhere. The shed wouldn't clean itself, so she grabbed the stuffed-full garbage bag and drug it to the dumpster.

That job done, the flowerbed beside the Jeb's Sugar Pine was next on her list. She sank the shovel into the weed-strewn flowerbed and flipped over a scoop of dirt. An earthworm wiggled in the dark soil, working its way out of the sunlight. There was no changing the past, but she could find a better future.

She'd reached mid-point of the flowerbed when the sound of a truck caught her attention. She looked over her shoulder to see Bose coming around the corner of the house.

Her lungs tightened, and her stomach did a fancy backflip. Would she ever get over the feeling of joy at the sight of him?

As he walked over to her, he pulled his cell phone from his jean's pocket and handed it to her. "Cary called. Willa wants to talk to you."

With no money for extravagances, Marlene had given up her cell when she'd moved back to East Hope. As she reached for the phone, her hand froze in mid air. "What will I say? Hi, baby. I'm your mom. I love you even though

I ran off and left you."

"Why don't you wait and see what she says before you jump to the worst conclusion." Bose took the phone, pushed a button and handed it back.

Marlene's heart beat so fast, she wasn't sure she'd be able to hear Willa when she answered. She needn't have worried. It was Cary who spoke. "Hello?"

Clearing her throat once and then again, Marlene tried to find the right words, any words.

Bose touched her cheek. "Say hello."

"Hello. Bose said Willa wanted to talk to me." On the verge of fainting and losing the connection, Marlene sank to the ground and leaned against the rough truck of the Sugar Pine. "I mean, if she doesn't, I understand."

What had seemed a pleasant, crisp fall day suddenly became stifling. Air got stuck on the way to her lungs, and a bead of sweat trickled down her neck. The iridescent gleam of a green bottle fly glowed in the sun as it landed on her knee. She didn't bother to flick it away. Breathing took what little focus she had left.

Bose stood a few feet away, a teasing grin on his rugged face. "If you pass out, you'll never know what she has to say."

Damn the man, he was right again. If Willa hated her, at least she'd know, and she could make a decision based on fact instead of fear. Marlene took a moment to clear her thoughts. "Cary, I'd like to see Willa."

Cary's calm voice came through the line. "I agree. Can you come out in the next couple of hours? She's leaving at five for volleyball practice."

Yes! Yes! Yes! Marlene wanted to shout she'd come out now, but she took a breath and concentrated until she could speak in a normal tone of voice. "Thank you, Cary. I'll be there as soon as I can get ready." She disconnected and handed the phone back to Bose.

He stuck the cell into his pocket then resettled his East Hope Equipment Salvage cap onto his head. "What's the plan?"

Marlene let her gaze roam around the place. The barn was timeworn, but it was solid. The house was a double wide, but it was cozy and sound. Her truck was old, but it ran. This is not the place she would have seen herself a few years ago, but today, it looked pretty good.

If things were different, and they would have been if she hadn't ruined every relationship she'd ever been in, she'd love to stay here. Bose watched her as the random thoughts ran through her brain. She gave him a slight smile. "Plan? Run a brush through my hair and drive to Micah's to face my daughter."

"I know that. Got any idea what you're going to say?" Bose followed her to the house.

When they were inside, Marlene turned to him. He'd voiced the question she'd put to herself every day for the last three years. No matter how hard she thought the answer was always the same. "I have no idea."

"Want me to go with you?" His smile gave her equal amounts of warmth and guilt.

How had she ever walked away from this man? "More than anything." She sank to the arm of the sofa and focused her gaze on the worn spot on the toe of her sneakers. "All you ever did was help me and take care of me, and I hurt you. I would give almost anything to undo the pain I caused. I'm working very hard to make you, Willa, and Wendy proud of me."

Bose put a fingertip beneath her chin and lifted until she looked him in the eyes. "For once in your life, why don't you make you proud. Willa might not forgive you today, but unless you screw things up again, she will soon." He ran his fingers through her short curls. "When did you decide to do this?"

"This morning. I guess I got carried away with my trim."

"I like it." He pulled on a curl then let it spring back. "Let's go talk to your daughter."

On a normal day, Marlene enjoyed the sight of the desert, the gnarled Junipers, and the giant sagebrush. Today, her mind was on Willa. The ten miles between Jeb's place and Micah's ranch passed in silence. Thoughts pinged around in her brain at the speed of light, ranging from a joyful reunion with her daughter to the girl saying she never wanted to see her mother again.

Bose turned into the driveway at the ranch house. Switching off the ignition, he turned to her. "You go on in. I'll wait here. Willa doesn't need a stranger listening in on your conversation."

Marlene's heart did a double flip before settling at the bottom of her stomach. She'd assumed Bose would come in with her, but he was right. She'd caused this, and she alone needed to clean it up.

She walked up the wide steps to the old oak front door, took a minute to gather her courage then before she could chicken out, she knocked. The clatter of children's feet and raised voices echoed through the front door.

"I got it! I got it!" A high-pitched voice called out, and the doorknob rattled.

"Rodie, let me open it." Her daughter's voice hadn't changed in the time she'd been gone. A second later Marlene was looking into the blue eyes that were a copy of her own. A small carbon copy of Micah stood in front of Willa.

Marlene had planned to keep her emotions in check until she figured out how Willa felt, but the wide smile spreading across her face had a mind of its own. "Hi, honey."

Willa knelt down in front of her brother. "Rodie, Ma said she had a cookie for you."

The little boy took another look at Marlene, gave her a quick grin, and raced for the kitchen.

Willa stood and looked at her mother. The smile she'd had for her brother collapsed into a frown.

"You call Cary Ma?" She tried to keep the envy from

her voice. Willa's favorite TV show had been *Little House On The Prairie*, and the girl had insisted on calling her parents Ma and Pa. Marlene had hated it at the time, and had refused to answer. Now, she'd have given—she'd have given anything to reach back in time and change her reactions.

Willa tilted her head, her eyes narrowing as she answered. "Yes, she likes it."

Since the moment Cary had called and invited her to talk to Willa, a little voice in the back of Marlene's brain had been screaming this wasn't a good idea. Was this a set-up by Micah? Did he want to see her humiliated one more time? No. Even thought Micah hated her, he was a kind person, and he would never do anything to hurt Willa.

She looked back at Bose sitting in the truck. Because of the sun's glare on the windshield, she couldn't see him clearly, but she imagined him giving her a thumbs-up. Paranoia was going to have to find another place to live, because she wasn't going to invite it in any more. She grinned. "Hi, Willa."

A slow smile changed her daughter's face from anxious to beautiful. "You cut your hair."

That was what the frown had been about? "Yes, I did. What do you think?" She ran her fingers through the short spikes. Did Willa hate her short hair? The screen door between them kept her from reading her daughter's expression.

More than anything, Marlene wanted to pull Willa into her arms and cover her with kisses, but for the moment, she'd lost that right. She'd talk about hair instead until they found more solid ground.

"It's not like mine anymore, but it's okay." Willa pushed the door open and walked out onto the porch. "Who's in the truck?"

Marlene couldn't take her eyes off her daughter. She'd grown from a little girl to a young lady in the time she'd been gone. When Willa turned, she noticed the bits of grass clinging to her daughter's curls and a smudge of dirt on her arm. Maybe using *Willa* and *lady* in the same sentence was stretching it a little. "That's a friend of mine. Bose Kovac."

"You're leaving with him." It was a statement, not a question. The frown was back, magnified by a power of ten.

The words stopped Marlene in her tracks. Of course Willa would think she'd found another man. It was the only behavior her mother had ever shown. "No, he's only a friend, honey. Just a friend."

"But you are leaving, right?"

Marlene couldn't think of a way to explain that no matter how much she longed to stay, she couldn't. She'd burned that bridge. She didn't belong here, would never be accepted here. "I honestly don't know."

Willa's eyes brimmed with tears, and she wiped them away with a quick motion. Her little jaw set in a move exactly like Micah when he was angry. She stalked to the front door and looked over her shoulder as her hand settled on the handle. "Pa said you wouldn't stay—even for me."

STEPHANIE BERGET

# CHAPTER EIGHT

Bose couldn't hear what was being said, but it was obvious Marlene's meeting with her daughter wasn't going well. Willa stormed back into the house, slamming the door. Marlene's shoulders slumped. She sank into the closest Adirondack chair. With her face buried in her hands, she sat motionless.

Bose opened the truck door and had one foot on the ground when the front door opened, and Micah's wife came out. She stood next to Marlene and put her hand on the other woman's shoulder.

By their gestures they as they spoke, Bose knew they weren't making cordial chitchat. He'd started toward the house when Marlene stormed off the porch and ran to the truck. "Get me out of here."

Bose looked back at Cary. The woman didn't look angry. She looked sad. The door to the passenger side slammed shut, and he climbed in before Marlene slid across the seat and drove away without him.

When they reached the highway, Bose pulled over at the first turnout. He switched off the key and turned to Marlene. "Want to talk?"

She whirled to face him, her hands clenched into fists

on her thighs. "Why are you so nice to me?" Bright, pink spots colored her cheeks, and her breathing came in rapid puffs. She ran her fingers through her hair, leaving it in uneven spikes. "You, more than anyone, should know I'm not worth the time it takes to get to know me."

Bose ignored her statement. He pulled a bottle of water from beside the seat. It wasn't cold, but it was all he had. "What did your daughter say?" He twisted the top off and handed it to Marlene. "Drink."

She took a small swallow then tipped the bottle, pouring a bit onto her fingers. With a sigh, she patted the water onto her face. When she'd finished, she wiped off her mouth with the back of her hand and gave him the bottle back. "She wants me to stay. How can I explain to her that I can't? Nothing I can say, especially the truth, will make it okay."

Bose stared out the window. Marlene was right. There was no easy answer, but if he knew one thing, it was that life was never easy. You just had to do the best you could with the hand you were dealt. He turned to face her. "Well, then stay here. You've got a place to live." Staying in East Hope would be one of the hardest things Marlene ever did, but she was tough. If she set her mind to it, she could do this. He almost wished he'd be around to help, but this wasn't his problem. "Stay and make things right."

"I promised Micah I wouldn't come around. I'm trying really hard to keep my word." She looked into his eyes. "And, I don't have a place to live because I listed Jeb's place a couple of days ago."

"You need to decide what would be the best thing for your daughter. Not what Micah thinks is best, but what you think is best."

She flopped back in the seat and closed her eyes. "I think what's best for Willa is if I leave."

"If you think having your daughter wonder why her mother didn't care enough to stay is the best thing to do, then leave." He shifted his gaze out the front window, but watched her from the corner of his eye. "If you are determined to do the right thing with your life, do the right thing for your daughter, too."

Marlene rolled her head just far enough to make eye contact. "It's days like these that make me wish I still liked to drink. Can you take me home?"

Bose turned the knob of the radio. With music playing at least the silence in the truck cab wasn't as oppressive. When they pulled into the yard, Wendy was curled into Jeb's old lawn chair by the porch.

She sprang up and ran to Marlene. "Daddy was supposed to call me when I got home from school, and I haven't heard from him."

Bose glanced at his phone. Gerald was supposed to call over an hour ago. Tension tightened his shoulder muscles. Something was wrong. Wendy's father was never more than a few minutes late with his calls when he was on the road. "Did you try to call him?"

Wendy's lip quivered as she tried to hold back her tears. "Yes, three times. He didn't answer. I left him messages, too. He didn't call back."

Marlene put her arm around the girl's shoulders and led her to the house. "Come on. We'll find him. He's probably broken down somewhere where he doesn't get cell service."

Jeb's ragged, brown phone book was on the corner of the kitchen counter. Marlene flipped it open then pointing to Gerald's number, she handed it to Bose. "Will you try calling?"

The call went to voicemail. Either Gerald was out of service or—. He glanced into the book again. Beneath Gerald's number was the one for his employer.

The phone rang only twice before a professional, friendly voice answered. "Taylor Trucking. How can I help you?"

"I'm trying to find Gerald Wilson. He hasn't called his daughter, and she's getting worried." When the secretary put him on hold, a scratchy rendition of *Happy Days Are Here Again* played. Thank goodness it was only a minute before a man came back on the line.

"This is Charles Taylor. Can I ask who's calling?"

"I'm Bose Kovac. Marlene Clegg is taking care of Gerald's daughter when he's on the road."

"Gerald told me about Marlene taking Jeb's place with Wendy. He should be in Denver. Hold on a minute."

Bose could hear another person talking to Mr. Taylor as he waited, but he couldn't make out the words. When Taylor came back on the line, Bose asked, "Is everything all right?"

The man hesitated a moment too long before replying. "I'll need to call you back."

"Sure," Bose said, because what else could he say. As he hung up Jeb's phone, a small hand slipped into his. He smiled down at Wendy. He had a bad feeling about this, but didn't he want the girl to pick up on his anxiety. If there were any justice in this world, they'd all be able to laugh about their concerns later. "Your dad's boss is going to find out what's going on."

Marlene fixed hot chocolate and put on Wendy's favorite movie, but none of them could concentrate. Inch by inch, Wendy scooted closer to Marlene until she practically sat in her lap.

Had the battery in the clock had run down? If the hands were moving at all, they had to be running at half speed. An endless half hour passed before his phone rang. He smiled at Wendy and moved into the other room to answer.

"Charles Taylor here. We've just gotten word that Gerald was involved in an accident. He's in surgery at St. Luke's Medical Center in Denver. From the little I've been able to find out, he's pretty badly hurt. I've left a message for the doctor to call me as soon as there's word on his condition. I'm sorry I don't have better news."

The man continued to talk, telling Bose the few details

available. Bose's thoughts flashed to Wendy. For a kid who'd lost her good friend Jeb recently, this was going to be doubly hard. The silence on the other end of the line brought him back to the present. "Thanks, Mr. Taylor. We'll wait to hear from you." He hung up and took a minute to collect his thoughts.

What was he supposed to say to Wendy? That her dad was going to be fine, or that he didn't know anything yet. But in the end he decided Wendy was a smart kid, and she deserved to know the truth.

The girl rounded the corner, her eyes wide, her lips quivering. Marlene stood right behind her, a hand on her shoulder. "What's wrong?" Wendy's normally cheerful face was pasty with fear.

Bose took her hand and led her to the living room. He sat on the couch, and she dropped down beside him. "Your dad was in an accident."

Some of the girl's tension faded. "He's gonna be mad if some jerk ran into his truck and wrecked it." Wendy leaned back against the sofa, a relieved smile on her lips. "He loves his truck almost as much as he loves me."

"It's not the truck. Your dad wanted to get something to eat at a truck stop outside of Denver. Someone sped through the parking lot and hit him as he stepped out from behind his truck."

The light in Wendy's eyes evaporated along with her blossoming hope. She wrapped her arms around herself and rocked back and forth.

"How bad is he?" Marlene sat beside Wendy and pulled the girl into her arms.

"We don't know yet. He's in surgery. Mr. Taylor is going to call as soon as he learns anything." He wasn't accustomed to feeling helpless. Through sheer determination, he'd managed to fix any problems he'd encountered during his life. Even when Marlene had married another man, he'd thrown himself into becoming the best farrier the west coast had ever known. But this . . .

He didn't know how to fix this.

*~*

Bose had been on the phone trying to find flights to Denver when the second call from Mr. Taylor came through. Marlene could see from the expression on his face the news wasn't good.

Before he had a chance to explain, his cell rang again. He listened for a moment then handed the phone to Marlene.

"It's Micah."

She didn't have the time or the energy to go toe-to-toe with her ex-husband over their daughter right now. She walked into the next room to take the call so the conversation wouldn't worry Wendy. "I'm a little busy."

"I know. What can we do to help?"

His concern sounded genuine, but how had he found out this quickly? "How? Where?"

"Millie called. Apparently, at one time, Gerald had put her as a contact with his company if there were ever any problems. The secretary just called. She didn't have any details. Is it bad?"

Marlene's throat closed tight, and she struggled to breathe. She concentrated on pulling in slow breaths, but it didn't do much good. When she could finally speak, the sentences were choppy and disorganized. "I think—I think it's bad. We're—Bose is trying to find a flight." She cleared her throat. "Find a flight to Denver."

"If you need someone to watch the place or feed the animals, Clinton has offered. What can Cary and I do to help?"

She should have known. Even with all the bad feelings between her and her ex-husband, he wouldn't ignore Wendy. The people in this town were amazing. She'd lived in paradise and hadn't realized it. "Micah, can I call you back. We just got the news."

"Sure. We'll be waiting to hear from you." Marlene had almost disconnected when she heard Micah's voice again. "Anything, Marlene. If you need money for the trip or anything else, let us know."

When Marlene walked back into the living room, Bose had his arms around a sobbing Wendy. He set her onto the sofa and knelt in front of her. "There's nothing we can do right this moment for your dad. I'm going to take us all to Denver. I know it's hard, but we need to think positive. What would Jeb have said?"

Wendy sniffled. "No sense crying over spilt beer."

"And he was right. I can see Bomber with her head hanging over the fence. It's past time for her grain."

Wendy looked from the horse to Bose. She nodded her agreement and left without another word.

Marlene watched as the girl trudged across the lawn, climbed over the fence and buried her face in Bomber's mane. She turned to Bose. "What did they say?"

"It's not good," Bose said. "He has a broken leg and a concussion. But the worst part is the injuries to his kidneys and liver. They're not sure if he's going to make it."

Marlene closed her eyes, trying to control her emotions. It wouldn't do Wendy any good to watch her fall apart. When she opened them, she turned toward her bedroom. "I'll start packing. Let me know when you find the tickets to Denver. Micah said he'd loan me the money to pay for them."

The concern on Bose's face faded. The muscle on his jaw twitched. Tension flowed off him and hit her like a tidal wave. "Maybe you'd be better off asking Micah to go with you."

What the hell? Why would she want her ex-husband? She shook her head. She didn't have the time or brainpower to figure out Bose's change of attitude now. She placed her hand on his arm. "Wendy and I need you. Please come with us." When he nodded, she said, "I'm going to pack."

"Marlene?"

She looked up to see anger, or was that disappointment on his face.

"I can pay for the tickets." He turned his back and pulled his phone out of his pocket.

She'd hurt Bose's feelings again. Maybe on the ride to the airport, she could apologize. Hurrying next door, she packed several outfits for Wendy. By the time she got back to the mobile home, Bose had arranged tickets for early the next morning, leaving from Boise. He'd also reserved a motel room in Boise and Denver.

Marlene grabbed a few things for herself while Bose went to pack. By the time he got back, she and Wendy were waiting on the front steps.

Bose stacked their suitcases in the backseat of the truck, and they began the four-hour trip to the motel in Boise. Wendy curled up in the back seat, and stared at Bose's iPad.

Marlene didn't think the girl saw a thing moving across the screen. The fear and misery on Wendy's face broke her heart.

There was nothing she could do about Wendy right now, but she could talk to Bose. "I don't know what I said back at the house to make you angry, but I'm sorry."

His jaw tensed and his lips thinned. They rode for a few minutes before he spoke. "You didn't do anything." His face moved into what might have been a grin.

"Then what?"

"I can pay for the tickets and whatever else you need. You don't have to go begging for money to your ex-husband."

"I didn't—" Before she got herself into more trouble, she cut off what she'd been going to say. Was Bose jealous of Micah? She couldn't imagine that. There was nothing to be jealous about. "Thanks, Bose. Micah offered, and I didn't think." And men say women are hard to understand. "I don't know what Wendy and I would have done if you weren't here."

After a drive that seemed to go on forever and a sleepless night, they were even more on edge. By the time they had made it through the early morning security check and were waiting to be called for boarding, Marlene felt like she was at the end of her rope. She couldn't imagine what Wendy felt like.

The girl was pale and quiet, so unlike the joyful child she'd come to know.

The flight would have been under two hours without the layover and a minor mechanical problem with the plane. As it was, it took eight. Bose checked every hour, but there had been no change in Gerald's condition.

Even with the flight delay, they were at the hospital before any of them were ready to face reality. Bose locked their bags in the pickup then he and Marlene accompanied Wendy into the hospital.

An elderly woman at the entrance told them how to get to the Intensive Care Unit. As they maneuvered the long curving hallways, the sterile scent of the hospital turned Marlene's stomach, and she held Wendy's hand a little tighter.

Marlene's heart pounded against her chest as they neared the nurse's station. A woman dressed in pale blue scrubs looked over the tall counter and smiled. "Can I help you?"

"This is Wendy Wilson," Marlene said. "She's here to see her father, Gerald."

"Where's my daddy?" Wendy's voice was edged in panic, and her gaze jumped from room to room.

"I'll show you where he is, honey." The nurse stopped in front of Wendy. "He's asleep right now. Don't be too worried if he doesn't talk to you." She led them to a room across the hall and opened the door.

The soft sounds of the machines set Marlene's nerves on edge. She'd do anything to spare Wendy this pain, but if she'd learned anything it was that each person had to live with and learn from what life threw at them.

Wendy stopped in the doorway, her eyes wide as she stared at her father. His normally tanned face was as white as the pillowcase, and his breathing was so slow, Marlene found herself watching to make sure he took the next one. The girl moved across the room, her shoes dragging against the shiny linoleum.

Marlene followed Wendy to the bed. As she pulled the little girl close, she felt each of Wendy's shuddering breaths pass through her body.

"Daddy. I'm here." Wendy reached out a hand and touched her father's arm, but he didn't move. She turned her tear-tracked face to Marlene. "What if he dies?"

How could she reassure this child when she didn't even know for sure what she'd be doing next week? She ran her fingers across Wendy's forehead and tucked a strand of hair behind her ears. "We'll figure it out as we go."

"Mama's gone, Jeb went to heaven, and if Daddy dies, I'll be all alone."

A lump the size of Jeb's Sugar Pine formed in Marlene's throat at the fear in Wendy's voice. "No, you will never be alone. You'll have me as long as you need me."

"And me."

Bose's deep voice gave her a sudden surge of hope, but as she glanced down at Wendy, it faded away as quickly as it had appeared. Marlene had been a spectacular failure when it came to raising her own daughter. What guarantee was there that she'd do better with this girl?

She took a breath to steady her brain. There must be some family members somewhere who'd love to have this sweet child. She only had to be up to the task of caring for Wendy until her father was well or an aunt or uncle was found.

A nurse hurried into the room, the soles of her shoes producing a tiny squeak with each step. "I'll bet you could use a break. The cafeteria is in the basement." She smiled at Wendy then looked at Marlene. "Come back in about ten minutes."

"Let's go get something hot to drink." Bose started toward the door, but Wendy hung back.

"I don't want to leave Daddy."

The nurse gave her another warm smile. "I have to change his bandages. Give me a few minutes then you can stay as long as you want." Wendy studied the woman for a moment before nodding in agreement.

Marlene took her hand, and they walked to the elevator.

"Is Daddy going to die?"

Marlene's vow to always tell the truth had never been harder to maintain, but she had a feeling this smart little girl would sense if she lied. "I don't know, honey, but I promise you, Bose and I will be with you always." She glanced at Bose, and he gave her a small smile. At least she wasn't in this alone.

Wendy's small body shook with sobs. When the elevator opened in the basement, Marlene led Wendy to a bench in a small alcove. As Wendy threw her skinny arms around Marlene's neck, she held the girl as both their hearts broke.

# CHAPTER NINE

Bose carried the drinks from the cafeteria, giving himself another mental head slap as he walked. What the hell was he thinking? Twice now he'd agreed to stay with Wendy and Marlene until Wendy's situation was stable. He had to learn to quit promising things he wasn't sure he could do.

Six short months was what he'd promised Jeb when he'd agreed to take care of the old man's clients. He'd said he'd stay that long or until another horseshoer could be found.

His goal all along had been to set up shop in an area filled with rich people and their expensive horses. If he was going to excel at a job that was as physically demanding as being a farrier, he was damned sure going to get paid for his effort.

He rounded the corner to see the little redhead sitting on Marlene's lap. When he looked at Wendy's tear-stained face, his frustration faded into nothingness. There was no way he could abandon this kid. He hurried down the hallway and handed a hot chocolate to Wendy. The girl stared into the cup, but Bose didn't see her take a drink. At least, she'd gotten control of her tears, for now. The haunted look was still there, but when she stood, some of the old Wendy was back. "It's been long enough. Can we go see Daddy?"

Bose dumped the cups into the trash. The elevator opened as they walked up, and before they had time to turn around, they'd arrived on the second floor.

Unease wrapped around Bose, sending sharp stabs of apprehension racing down his arms. Gerald had been pale and lifeless, and Bose hoped the man hadn't died while they'd been gone. Was that why the nurse had urged them to leave?

It was a relief to see Gerald still in his bed, still breathing albeit shallow and slow.

Wendy watched him for a few moments almost as if she were afraid to touch him. Finally, she walked up to his side and wrapped his unencumbered hand in both of hers. "Wake up, Daddy."

The bandage on Gerald's forehead was crisp and white, but an angry red scratch ran the length of his neck. One of his eyes was swollen shut, but he opened the other one, and looked at Wendy. Pulling in a shallow, ragged breath, he made an effort to smile. "Hey, baby girl."

Wendy, along with Marlene, gasped in surprise.

Bose was pretty sure he gasped, too.

A smile brighter than the sun spread across the little girl's face and tears filled her eyes. "Hi, Big Daddy. Are you okay?"

Bose could see how hard it was for Gerald to return his daughter's smile, but the man put on a good show.

"I'm doin' fine. Aren't you supposed to be in school?" Gerald coughed then grimaced, his free hand moving to his chest. It took a moment before he could speak again. "How am I ever going to retire if you don't graduate and get a good job?"

This was a conversation Bose had heard between the elder and younger Wilsons many times. Gerald was doing everything he could to make Wendy's world normal in a horribly abnormal situation.

"Daddy, we came as soon as we found out where you were." Tugging softly at his blanket, she smoothed out the wrinkles. Her hands fluttered around the pillow, and she carefully touched the unbandaged side of his face. "I was really scared when you didn't call." The last couple of words faded to a whisper then she straightened and cleared her throat. "I can't let you out of my sight, can I?"

"Hey," Gerald said then closed his good eye and took slow measured breaths. When he opened it again, his pain seemed to have faded. "I'm supposed to say that to you."

Bose had heard this exchange often, too.

Marlene had moved to lean against the wall by the door, her hands wrapped around her body, her face pale. She shifted her gaze from Wendy and her father to Bose and attempted to give him a smile. She failed.

"Baby girl, I need to talk to Marlene for a moment. I don't suppose you and Bose could go find me a glass of orange juice, could you?"

Wendy turned to look at Bose, and he nodded and walked with her out into the hall. The nurse at the ICU desk smiled at Wendy as she approached. "My daddy wants some orange juice."

The woman glanced at Bose before looking back at Wendy. "I'm sorry, he's not allowed anything but ice chips."

Wendy turned back to him, uncertainty making her frown, and he managed a smile. "Then, we'll take the very best ice chips you have."

The nurse pointed toward the lounge. A small icemaker sat in the corner. A juice machine stood along side. The nurse handed Wendy a cup. "Now, remember. He can't have orange juice just yet. You can give him ice whenever he wants some."

Wendy filled the cup, and led the way back to the room, holding the Styrofoam cup in both hands like a gift. "Big Daddy, I brought you ice. The nurse says this will help you get better."

Gerald's face was pinched in pain, and his breath rasped in and out of his lungs in a slow dirge. He tried to say something to Bose, but collapsed onto the pillow. The short visit had obviously worn him out, and his eye slid shut.

Wendy crawled with infinite care onto the edge of the bed and laid her head on the pillow beside her father.

When Bose turned to Marlene, her skin was nearly as pale as Gerald's. He gave her a questioning look, and she jerked her chin toward the door.

"We'll be outside, honey," Marlene told the girl. When they reached the lounge, Marlene turned to face him. Her hands shook as she handed Bose the folded paper she'd been holding. Without a word, she dropped into a chair by the door.

"What's this?" Bose raised his gaze to hers, but she just shook her head. If this had been good news, she'd have come right out and told him. He had a sick feeling in the pit of his stomach.

"Read it."

When she refused to look at him, he unfolded the paper and began reading. "What the hell!" He managed to keep his voice quiet, but he couldn't stop the words from rushing out. This could not be happening.

The antiseptic scent of the hospital became nauseating, and he swallowed hard. "Gerald gave you this?"

"He had it written up and a nurse and the chaplain signed as witnesses." She shook her head keeping her gaze glued to her scuffed boots. "You are no more shocked than I am."

"This isn't legal, is it?"

"I don't know for sure, but I bet it is."

"Well, he has to take it back. He can't will his daughter to us." Bose paced the small room, his mind whirling in confusion. "I'm not— I can't—"

Marlene exploded out of her chair and stalked toward

him. "Do you think I can? Hell, my own daughter won't talk to me, and he wants . . ." Her voice dropped to a whisper, and she looked at him for the first time. "We don't have any choice."

"I do. There must be someone else."

The glare Marlene gave him summed up her condemnation of his decision. She walked closer until she stood right in front of him. Her index finger poked him in the chest. "You're right." She poked him again. "You have a choice." One more poke. "You've got a life, and we wouldn't want anything or anyone dragging you down." As she finished scolding him, her anger seemed to fade away. Her hands dropped to her sides, and she turned to stare out the window at the bumper-to-bumper traffic on the street below

"But, doesn't she have any other family?" He'd never seen anyone around, but that didn't mean there wasn't family somewhere who'd love to have the girl.

"Gerald loves Wendy with every fiber of his being. Do you think he would give custody to two virtual strangers if he had anyone else he trusted?"

Bose's heart dropped. He opened his mouth to tell Marlene he'd help her with this as long as he was in town, when a nurse hurried into the room.

"Wendy needs you." She motioned for them to follow her and raced back down the hallway.

As they rounded the corner, he saw Wendy standing by the nurse's station, her head hanging. When she saw them, she raced toward them, nearly climbing into Marlene's arms. "Something happened to Daddy. They won't let me back in." A sob tore from the girl's throat, and Marlene gathered her close.

Bose took both of them to the nearest waiting room. Minutes ticked by with the speed of a snail in super glue, but when the doctor entered, Bose wished they'd had more time.

The doctor looked past Marlene and Wendy to Bose.

"The damage was too great. I'm sorry, he didn't make it."

Shock coursed through his veins. He'd known Gerald was badly hurt, but the big man had seemed indestructible. It didn't seem possible that Wendy's father was gone.

He looked at the little girl sobbing in Marlene's arms.

Wendy was his first priority now.

\*~\*

Wendy tucked the yellow stuffed horse daddy had given her when she was little beneath her chin and drew herself into a fetal position. It was the only thing that helped her sleep. She closed her eyes and tried to clear her mind, but all she could do was miss her father. Crawling out from under the covers, she pulled her bathrobe over her arms. It was purple with her name and a horse stitched on the pocket, her daddy's gift to her last Christmas. Pulling it tight around her body, she tied the belt, pretending it was a hug.

The full moon shone bright through the windows, and a gentle breeze shook the branches of the Sugar Pine. Bomber stood by the fence looking at the house, so she slipped out the back door. Bomber was her horse now. Just before her father had left for his last trip, Bose had asked if it was okay for Wendy to have the mare.

Her daddy had said yes.

At the time, she thought she'd never be sad again, but she should have known. Everyone she loved left sooner or later. She sometimes wondered what she'd done wrong, why people didn't stick with her.

She wound her arms around Bomber's neck and buried her face in the mare's black mane. "Daddy's not coming home ever again."

The mare blew warm sweet breath onto Wendy's face and stood very still. Wendy was sure the mare knew how sad she was. One thing helped though. She'd been wrong at the hospital. She wasn't alone. She had Bomber and

Marlene and Bose.

Even if Marlene sold Mr. Jeb's place, they could live at her house. Wendy reminded herself to transfer the plants to her daddy's house when they moved.

Everything would work out if she could convince Bose to stop looking for a job far away.

"Why don't you come in, honey? I fixed oatmeal with apples and cinnamon." Marlene's voice floated to her on the early morning air, the sound of safety in a scary world.

Wendy burrowed deeper into Bomber's mane. Even Marlene couldn't get her out of the memorial today, and the thought of seeing all those people made her stomach twitch and twist.

She wanted all this to go away.

She wanted things to go back to normal.

She wanted her daddy back.

*~*

Marlene knew wishing never got a person anywhere, but she wished with all her heart that she could make this transition easier for Wendy. From the time the girl's mother had left, and probably before, Wendy and her father had been as close as two people could be.

Wendy had been too quiet at the memorial, and Bose suggested they go home as soon as it finished.

Wendy came out of the bedroom at Jeb's where she'd slept since they'd come home from Denver. "Can I go ride Bomber?"

"Do you want me to saddle up Louie and go with you?" Bose and Wendy stood by the dining room window looking out at the pasture. "Louie needs a ride."

Wendy shook her head. "Nah. I need to talk to Bomber."

Marlene and Bose stood side by side and watched Wendy catch the old mare. "I don't know what to do. I'm not good at this," Marlene said.

"You're not the only one. At least you've been around a kid before. This is all new for me." He poured a cup of coffee and sat at the table where he could watch Wendy and the mare.

Marlene leaned against the bar and asked the question that had troubled her since the moment Gerald had died. "You're not staying in East Hope, right?"

Bose looked at her, his eyebrows raised in question.

"Because that sounds like you're staying, and you said you wouldn't. Did you change your mind?" She'd had all the surprises she could handle and needed to get this out in the open once and for all.

Bose took a sip of coffee then stared into his cup. "I've applied for a job I'd be a fool to pass up. If I get it, I'll have to go, but until then, I'm all yours."

"Don't put yourself out. We'll be fine without you. Wouldn't want to upset your plans." Marlene grabbed a pitcher from the cupboard and filled it before storming to the plant room.

She stopped and leaned against the wall. It was stupid to get mad. Bose had made it clear he wasn't in this for the long haul, and she didn't blame him. Fear was making her lash out, and she needed to stop over-reacting.

She carefully measured the water and gave each plant a drink. It wouldn't be too long before they were ready to harvest. Tomorrow she'd call Jeb's friend and get some advice.

"What do you want from me?" At the sound of his quiet voice, she jumped. Bose stood in the doorway, his fingers in the front pockets of his Wranglers. "I'm in a small rental. I don't make enough money to buy a place here. I never intended to stay, you know that."

Marlene focused on the plant in front of her. She knew everything he said was true, but she'd hoped for a miracle—for both herself and for Wendy. Gerald had given custody of Wendy to both of them, but they could walk away. Well, she couldn't. Not after watching the gregarious, out-spoken girl fall apart.

"Nothing, Bose." She placed the pitcher on the table and turned to face him. "I'm not being sarcastic. I know you have plans. It would be great if you'd call sometimes and talk to Wendy about her horse."

He frowned. "I'm not leaving yet."

She watched him standing there, everything she wanted and knew she couldn't have. Why had she been so stupid all those years ago? It was water under the bridge now, and no amount of hoping was going to change anything. She pulled herself up straighter. "Maybe you should. It'll be worse for Wendy if she gets used to you being here and then you leave." It would be much harder on Marlene, too.

He watched her, his dark eyes seeing into her soul. After too long, he nodded again. "If you think that's best. Let me know if you need anything, anything at all."

Her lips felt stiff from tension as she tried to smile. "We won't. It's been nice seeing you again, Bose."

"Marlene, I hope you find what you want." Bose lingered in the doorway. "Have a good life."

When he'd disappeared from the doorway, she sank to the floor. She was going to miss that man. More than miss. When had her feelings for Bose turned to love?

This was not what she'd planned. Now, she knew how he'd felt, only he hadn't left her for another woman, he'd left her for a damned job.

No matter how much it hurt, the right thing was to make him leave now. She kept repeating this mantra until an even more depressing thought occurred to her. She'd wondered if his feelings for her were as strong as hers for him. Now she knew the answer. They couldn't be, or he wouldn't have walked away this easily.

She'd worked hard to change the way she lived her life. She'd thought the change would make life easier. Boy had she been stupid.

Marlene pulled herself to her feet and wandered out to the kitchen. Bose stood in the yard talking to Wendy. As she watched, he gave the girl a hug, got into his truck and drove away taking a piece of her heart with him.

Wendy watched until he was out of sight then took her bridle off Bomber. She hung it on the fence and came to the house. Marlene held out her arms, and Wendy rushed into them.

"Bose is leaving."

"I know, but I'm not." Marlene laid her head on Wendy's hair. The scent of little girl wrapped around her, a wonderful reminiscence of Willa. She leaned back and smiled at Wendy. "I know what we need to do. Change your jeans. We're going to visit someone." Marlene hurried to the bathroom and ran a brush through her curls. She'd cut her hair in a fit of pique. Looking at the short curls now, she realized she liked her hair this way.

When she got back to the living room, Wendy was sitting where she'd left her, in the same dusty pants. "I don't want to go visit anyone." With her arms crossed and her chin down, she was the very picture of defiance.

Marlene sat down beside her. "I'm asking you to do me a favor. I want to introduce you to my daughter. She's mad at me, and I thought with you helping me, she might listen to what I have to say."

Wendy tried to maintain her attitude, but Marlene could see curiosity was winning out. "I didn't know you had a daughter." The girl raised her gaze to meet Marlene's. "Do I know her?"

Marlene scooted closer to Wendy and put her arm around Wendy's shoulder. "Maybe. Her name is Willa Wild West."

Wendy drew back and stared. "I know her, but you're not her mama."

The hits just kept coming. At least telling the truth, she didn't have to remember which story she'd told to which person. "I'm Willa's mom. I was married to Micah a long time ago."

"Are you Rodie's mom, too?" Wendy pulled her legs

underneath her.

"No. Cary is Rodie's mom. Look, I'll explain this all to you one of these days. Will you go with me?"

# CHAPTER TEN

Bose had spent all afternoon going through his tools, cleaning and sharpening, doing anything to keep his thoughts off Wendy and Marlene. He felt like a two-bit ass telling Marlene he couldn't promise to stay forever, but he'd had a plan for his life and the side-trip to East Hope had already set him back longer than he'd planned. As soon as the call from the exclusive Gold Medal Dressage Stables in southern California came through, he was gone.

He'd done his research, and Gold Medal was the premier stable in the western United States. With all that had happened, the perfect job didn't seem so perfect anymore.

He placed the last rasp back into the metal holder. When his work tools were in place in his truck, he turned his attention to the inside. With a whiskbroom, he swept out the dust on the floorboards. As he began spraying all-purpose cleaner on the dashboard, his cell rang.

He didn't recognize the number. "Kovac's Shoeing."

"Bose, it's Marlene."

Like he wouldn't recognize the voice he'd spent years fantasizing about. "It didn't take you long to call. You only kicked me out a couple of hours ago." He knew she was right about him leaving, but he'd earned the right to be bitter for a little while.

"It's Bomber. She's acting funny."

When he'd known Marlene before, she'd have come up with an excuse like this to keep stringing him along. He didn't think she'd do that now, and he couldn't risk Bomber. "I'll be right over."

Old habits died hard, and during the drive to Jeb's, he wondered again if Marlene was working on his emotions. As he rounded the corner of Jeb's trailer, he saw Wendy walking the mare, and he knew. Marlene would never use the girl to get to him. He climbed out and hurried over. "What's going on?"

Wendy's face was pale. "Bomber is sick. She wants to lay down all the time, and she bites at her flanks. I don't want her to die, too."

As Bose watched, the mare reached back and nipped at her side. Sweat spots darkened her neck. He hurried to his truck and pulled out a bottle and syringe. Looking at Marlene, he jerked his chin toward the house. "Find Doc Myers' number and tell him we need him now."

Marlene looked at him for a moment then took off toward the house at a run.

Bose prepared the injection, and Wendy brought the mare over to the fence. "This is like aspirin. It'll make her feel better."

While they waited for the vet, they took turns walking the mare to keep her on her feet. As the medication took effect, Bomber relaxed and became more comfortable.

At the sound of a truck coming down the driveway, Bose sent Wendy to show the vet the way.

"Thanks for dropping everything and coming to help," Marlene said. "I didn't know who else to call."

"How did you call? You don't have a phone." Bose watched as Marlene fished a small flip phone out of her pocket and handed it to him. "Where'd you get this?"

"It's a prepaid phone. I figured since I had Wendy here,

I needed something in case of emergencies. It came yesterday." She took the phone back and opened it. "It's cheap enough if I only use it for important calls."

The vet's truck rounded the end of the mobile home and pulled up to the fence. Wendy followed at a run.

"Hey, Doc."

Doc Myers smiled and walked up to the mare. "What's going on with Bomber?"

"Looks like colic."

Wendy stood beside Bose as the vet examined Bomber. "The Banamine you gave her is doing its job. Her gut sounds are good. We'll keep an eye on her for the next twelve hours, but I think she just has a mild case." The man ran his hand down Bomber's side then gave her a pat. "Jeb sure had an eye for horses, didn't he?" He turned to Marlene. "You ever want to sell this mare, you let me know."

Wendy wrapped her arms around the mare's neck, her eyes wide.

"The mare belongs to Bose." Marlene smiled at Wendy. "You'll have to talk to him."

Louie nickered from where he was tied to the fence. It appeared he didn't like the idea of Bomber being sold any more than Wendy did.

Bose ran his fingers through Bomber's mane. "I did some trading with Marlene, and own her right now, but Wendy and I made us a deal. I get the colt the mare's carrying, but Bomber belongs to Wendy."

The vet looked at Wendy and smiled. "You've got yourself a great little mare there. You take good care of her." He waved goodbye with instructions to call if they had any more problems.

"What do we do now, Bose?" Wendy rubbed the mare between the eyes then gave her a kiss on the nose. "What if she gets sick again?"

The worried look on Wendy's face made Bose's stomach drop. The last thing the girl needed was to lose the mare, too. But he owed her the truth. "The vet doesn't think this is serious. He's a good vet. We need to trust him. We'll keep watch on her tonight. If she's fine by morning, I think we'll be okay."

He turned to Marlene. "Mind if I sleep on the couch tonight. Wendy and I can take turns checking on Bomber."

Marlene crossed her arms and gave him a look that told him he'd stepped in it again.

He thought back to what he'd said and couldn't find anything that would make her mad. "If you'd rather, I can sleep in my truck." He was surprised she was being this stubborn. Usually when it came to Wendy, Marlene would give up the world to make the little girl happy.

"What about me?" Her stern look morphed into a smile. "Don't I get to take a turn? She is still technically my mare, you know."

Except for the short hair, Marlene looked the same, but if he hadn't known better, he'd think an alien had taken over her body. A really nice alien. From learning about horses for Wendy to giving up her life for the fatherless girl, Marlene had met every challenge. "We'll all take turns."

"If you're going to stay, I can at least cook dinner. What do you two want?" Marlene brushed her hand down the old mare's face. "You are a sweetheart, aren't you?"

As Bose watched, the mare leaned closer to Marlene, and she scratched behind Bomber's ears.

Marlene had enough on her mind, and he knew one thing he could do to help. "How about I order pizza?"

"Oh, crap." She started toward the house then turned back when he called out.

"You don't like pizza all of a sudden?"

Wendy tugged at his sleeve. "I do."

Marlene grinned at the girl then looked at Bose. "Pizza's fine, but I forgot to call Cary."

She hurried toward the house, and he enjoyed the

simple pleasure of watching her walk away. He was going to miss that, among other things. He marveled at the way her old jeans and a simple T-shirt looked every bit as sexy as when she'd dressed in the most expensive clothes she'd been able to get her hands on. In fact, they looked better.

He turned back to Wendy. "Let's put Bomber in the pen by herself. We can see her from the kitchen window there."

Wendy led the old mare over and took off her halter. "This way if she doesn't feel good, Louie won't be able to bother her." As soon as she was turned loose, Bomber walked across the pen to stand by the fence near the gelding. For the first time in too long, Wendy laughed. "Well, she can move away if she wants."

Bose put his arm around Wendy's shoulder. "You did good calling me right away."

"It was Marlene's idea." Wendy looked up at him, her face screwed up in confusion. "I don't understand why Millie doesn't like her. She's really nice."

Bose bent and plucked a dry stem of grass and pulled it through his fingers, as if folding the stalk into ever-smaller pieces would magically bring the right words to his brain. He sat on the top step and pulled off his boots before looking at Wendy again. "Millie and Marlene had a disagreement a long time ago. I guess they haven't gotten over it yet."

"Marlene has. She said she hoped Millie would like her again one day. Is Millie mad because Marlene is Willa's mom?"

He shook his head and reached over to ruffle Wendy's hair. He'd been proud of the answer he'd come up with, but it hadn't fool Wendy for a moment. This kid was so smart he'd never get by with a generic answer. "I think that was between Marlene and Micah."

Marlene slid the door open and saved him from coming up with something appropriate for Wendy. "Did you order the pizza?"

Bose pulled out his phone and hit speed dial. At Marlene's raised eyebrows, he shrugged. "Go ahead and laugh. They're the easiest way to get a hot dinner."

"Do you run a tab?"

As he opened his mouth to answer, he heard the teenager at Mountain Pizza answer the phone. "What kind to you want?" he asked Marlene. Marlene grinned and nodded toward Wendy.

"Hawaiian," Wendy said. "Is that okay?"

"Anything for my girls."

The smile faded from Marlene's face, and she turned and walked back into the house. What the hell? He turned to Wendy. "Does Marlene like Hawaiian, too?"

"She likes chicken artichoke. What's an artichoke?"

Bose could tell by the grin on Wendy's face that she knew the answer. She wanted to see if he did. "You go help Marlene, smarty, and I'll order one of each."

Bose finished the call and found Marlene at the kitchen counter, making a salad. "There's pop in the fridge. Help yourself." She tore lettuce into bite-sized pieces then added a variety of vegetables along with cheese, olives and sunflower seeds.

He popped the top and took a long drink. "You had to call Cary? I thought you two weren't speaking."

Marlene finished the salad and put it into the refrigerator. She dropped ice into a glass and filled it from the tap. "She called me to see if I'd try to talk to Willa again. Willa's been upset since our conversation the other day. I was going to take Wendy with me. I thought it might do both girls good to get to know each other." She set the glass on the counter without taking a drink. "Maybe I'm wrong."

Before he could answer, she spoke again. "I misjudged Cary. She's a nice woman, and a great step-mom for Willa."

"Did you tell her?" Each day, Bose was more amazed at the changes Marlene had made in her life. Until recently, he'd have sworn people didn't change, but standing in front of him was living proof.

"I did just now."

*~*

The sound of slamming of car doors told Marlene her daughter was here. She glanced at her reflection in the chrome toaster and smoothed down an errant curl. Her heart beat against her ribs. For a moment, Marlene's head spun, but she pulled in a deep breath.

Cleggs didn't fall apart at the first sign of adversity. She fixed a smile on her face and met Cary and Willa at the door with Wendy beside her.

The girls eyed each other.

"Wendy, can you get the cookies and sodas? Cary and Willa, won't you have a seat?" That sounded like a line from a sitcom Uncle Jeb used to watch, but her independent thought process had shut down at the sight of Willa.

"Thanks for having us over, Marlene." Cary's smile looked genuine, and Marlene was struck again by the way honesty and integrity flowed off the other woman. No wonder Micah had fallen in love with her.

Willa settled next to Cary, her gaze wandering around the room. "How come you're living here?" She looked at Marlene, her small face rigid. "You used to say trailer houses were for losers."

"Willa! Don't be rude." Cary's words brought a pink flush to Willa's cheeks, but she continued to glare at Marlene.

"She's right, Cary. I used to say that all the time. What I didn't tell Willa was that I was raised in a singlewide trailer. My granny couldn't afford anything better."

Willa had shifted her gaze to a worn spot on the couch, but her gaze snapped up to Marlene at the admission.

"I was ashamed, and I thought if I acted like I was

something special, everyone would think I was. Boy, that idea backfired." Marlene leaned back in the chair and tried her best to appear relaxed. "This was my Uncle Jeb's home, and when he died, he left it to me. I like it."

Wendy stood in the doorway, a plate of cookies in her hands. "We both like it." Her chin stuck out in defiance as she walked across the room and set the plate in Willa's lap. "Have a cookie." She hurried over to Marlene and sat on the arm of the chair.

"She's living with you?" Willa stood, and the plate dropped to the floor. She ran out the door to the car. Cary stood, but Marlene put her hand out to stop her. "Let me go."

Willa sat in the passenger seat, her arms wrapped around her body, her chin on her chest. Marlene opened the driver's door and slid inside. A soft sniffle from her daughter was the only sound.

"I know I've disappointed you. I've disappointed most everyone who's ever known me, but letting you down makes me feel the worst." She paused, trying to put her flailing thoughts into some kind of order. "I don't expect you to forgive me."

"Why are you leaving again? Don't you like me?" Tears formed in Willa's eyes, and her face flushed with emotion.

"I was leaving because I didn't think I had a choice. I made a lot of people mad when I lived here before, and they want me gone." A puff of wind danced through the interior of the car and lifted a red curl from Willa's hair and blew it across her face. "You probably won't believe this, but I love you more than you'll ever know."

"Are you going to stay now?"

That was the question of the century. Marlene reached across and tucked the curl behind Willa's ear. "I'm staying, at least for a while, and I'd love to get to know you again."

"But Wendy is living with you?"

How did she answer this so Willa would know she wasn't being replaced? "You've heard about Wendy's daddy dying, right?" At Willa's nod, she continued. "Wendy doesn't have any family left."

"What about her mama?" Willa had relaxed a bit, and her tears had slowed. She'd always been an empathetic girl, and she couldn't help thinking about someone beside herself.

"Like you, her mama left, but she doesn't have her daddy or a great stepmother like you. Wendy is alone. Her daddy asked me to take care of her. Me and Bose." Marlene waited for the blow-up. Willa would never forgive her for staying for a stranger but not for her daughter.

Wendy came out the front door and walked to the car. She leaned in and looked at Willa. "Want to see my horse? She's kind of sick."

Willa looked from Marlene to Wendy then shrugged. "Sure. What kind of horse do you have?" She climbed out of the car and followed Wendy around the corner of the house.

Marlene slumped in relief. Why she'd been expecting a blow-up, she didn't know. Willa was one of the most laid back kids she'd ever known. A lot like Wendy.

As bad as Marlene was at this mothering thing, she'd hit the jackpot with these two amazing kids. Climbing out of the car, she looked up to see Cary standing on the porch.

"Thanks for sending Wendy out," Marlene called as she approached the house.

When they got inside, Cary turned to her. "I didn't. It was her idea."

*~*

It was hard for Wendy to look at Willa and maintain her smile, but she was trying. Jealousy made her want to yell at the other girl for being rude to her mother. Willa had everything. Everything Wendy dreamed of plus she was Marlene's daughter.

Willa would never be alone.

The fear of angering Marlene was what kept her mouth shut. Marlene had promised she was staying, but Wendy wasn't positive that was the truth. If she said something out of line to Willa, Marlene might get mad and leave.

She led Willa around the house to the horse pens, smiling despite her fear when she saw Bomber. One thing Willa didn't own was the best horse in the world.

Bose sat on the fence watching the mare, and as they approached, he gave her his special smile. She knew he was leaving, but he was here for now and that had to be enough.

"How's Bomber?" Wendy scrambled up beside him, pretending a happiness she didn't feel.

Willa stood on the ground, looking uncomfortable.

Wendy's father had taught her good manners, and she should have invited Willa to join them, but leaving the other girl standing on the ground was one small way to get back at her.

"Bomber looks better. It wouldn't hurt to walk her though." Bose looked down, and when he smiled at Willa, another little jab of envy coursed through Wendy. "Hi, Willa."

"Hi." The girl grinned at Bose for an instant then fixed her gaze on the horse.

Bose jumped easily off the fence. "Will you stay out here with Wendy while I check something in the house?"

Wendy watched as Bose walked away then grabbed her halter. "I've got to walk Bomber around the pasture. I guess you can come with me if you want." She led the mare along the side of the pasture down to the small creek that ran most of the year. When she stopped, she looked around to see Willa approaching.

"This is nice." The rock Willa had climbed on extended over the water, and she'd walked to the edge. "We have a creek, but it's bigger and farther from the house."

Resentment gushed through Wendy, and her anger

fought its way past her fear. "Everything you have is bigger and better, isn't it?" She slammed her mouth shut, forcing the other words down before she wrecked everything. Slumping to the ground, she fought tears. Bomber put her nose on the top of her head, but even the love of the old mare wasn't enough. She'd lost too much to fight any longer.

An image of Willa's red boots wavered through her tears. Wendy felt a hand on her shoulder. "I didn't mean to sound like I'm better than you."

"But it's true. You've got a ranch, and a daddy, and a stepmother, and a brother, and now Marlene wants you, too. There won't be room for me." Wendy had tried to be brave, but her heart couldn't take any more.

"I was jealous because Marlene wanted you more than me." Willa dropped to the ground beside Wendy. "We're both unhappy because of the same thing."

*~*

Bose watched as the girls led the mare toward the creek then stuck his head in the door. "How are things going in here?"

Marlene gave him a watery smile. "Everyone in this town, including my daughter hates me. Other than that, it's all good."

"She doesn't hate you." Cary grinned. "Well, she doesn't hate only you. She's twelve. She hates everyone most of the time."

Bose looked over his shoulder. "Wendy and Willa are out in the pasture with Bomber. I'm not sure if that's a good thing. Neither girl looked too happy." He moved to the couch and dropped down with a sigh. "Kids are complicated."

Marlene wiped the tears off her cheeks and managed a smile.

Even without makeup, she was the prettiest woman

he'd ever seen. He had the urge to gather her into his arms and comfort her, but he fought the impulse. Even if he was sure Marlene had changed, his life was planned out. It didn't include a family.

Marlene stood. "I'd better go talk to them. You two want to come with me?" The hopeful look on her face told him how scared she was of confronting the two girls.

"I think this is something you need to do without my interference," Cary said. "I'll wish you luck."

"Call me if they gang up on you." Bose had known by the look on Wendy's face she needed Marlene's reassurance. He couldn't give the girl what she wanted. He wasn't staying.

An uncomfortable silence filled the room as soon as Marlene left. "Want something to drink?" he finally asked, when he couldn't stand the tension another minute. He stood, but Cary waved a hand, telling him to sit back down.

"Mind if I ask you a question?"

"Sure." It was a lie. He wasn't sure about anything these days. There were about a thousand questions she could ask. They probably all involved Marlene, and he was sure he wouldn't want to answer any of them. "Fire away."

"Are you leaving?" Cary folded her hands in her lap.

"Have to." He did have to leave if he was going to keep his life on track.

"Why?"

"That's more than one question." How did he explain that he'd planned and worked for this opportunity, and even though he'd miss Wendy and Marlene, he couldn't give everything up on the chance Marlene was really a different person?

"Okay. It just seems strange to me. I see the way you look at Marlene, and Wendy seems important to you. I'll tell you from my own experience, there's nothing better than surrounding yourself with people who love you."

Bose couldn't think of a thing to say. He knew she was

right, but Marlene had shattered his heart once before. He couldn't give her another chance. "Got a job."

A small smile crept across Cary's face, and she shook her head. Pity flowed out of every cell in her body. "A job? Better be a good one to take the place of what you've found here."

Confusion made Bose strike out. "Why are you Marlene's champion? You had a first hand taste of how conniving she can be."

"Was. She's not that way now."

"How can you be sure?"

"I saw her before. Deception and greed were her motivating factors. She was only out for herself. Now, more than anything, she wants to be in Willa's life. But she'd also back away if that's what was best for her daughter. And she's willing to make a home for Wendy even though she's scared to death of screwing up again."

Bose stood and walked to the front door. He hesitated, trying to find the words to make Cary understand. Looking over his shoulder, he said the only thing he could. "I have to leave. Call Micah and have him come over. Wendy's horse had a mild case of colic earlier. Someone who knows horses should check her out every few hours."

The compulsion to get away had him nearly running to his truck. He jammed it into gear and sped down the highway. Cary had it all wrong. She'd seen Marlene at her worst, but she hadn't been in love with the woman, hadn't had her heart ripped out by Marlene's deceit.

The stop sign at the intersection of Jeb's road and the main highway offered him a choice. He could turn right and go home, or left into town. Right now, he needed a beer and his fridge was empty.

As if the drinking gods approved of his decision, he found one open spot in front of the bar. A stool at the far end was empty, and he claimed it. The semi-darkness encouraged his attitude, and the cryin' and dyin' country song filtering through the air fit his mood.

Solitude was going to be his new best friend, along with a whole bunch of Buds. Halfway through his fourth, or was it his sixth beer, he felt someone brush his sleeve.

Micah slid onto the stool next to him.

Shit! He didn't need advice from Marly's ex-husband. The last thing he wanted to do was compare scars.

Bose scanned the room to see if there was an empty table, but just his luck, as he'd sat here nursing his drinks, the bar had filled up. Time to make a break for home. He could pick up more beer on the way.

"Drinking your troubles away?" Micah waved at the bartender. "Let me buy you another one."

Bose stood and threw two twenty-dollar bills on the bar. "Gotta go." As he turned toward the door, he tangled his feet up with the leg of the barstool and nearly fell on his face. If Micah hadn't grabbed his arm, he'd have been the laughing stock of the bar.

"Sit down." Micah's expression told Bose the man wasn't kidding. "We need to talk."

He could walk out, ignore the man, but he had to live in this town, at least for a while. He slid back onto the bar stool and took another sip of the beer. He focused his gaze on the red glow of the Budweiser sign as it colored the elk horns hanging over the bar. If Micah wanted to chat, he was going to have to do all the talking.

"I don't usually butt into other people's business."

Bose turned slowly and glared to Micah. "So you picked me to practice on? How'd I get so lucky?" In another life, he could have liked Micah West. The man was cowboy through and through. Why he'd pick this time to interfere was a mystery Bose didn't want to think about.

"It's for my daughter. Well, my wife pushed me into it, but she's doing it for my daughter. Marlene moving back to town has been a shock for all of us. Willa was delighted until she found out her mother wasn't staying." Micah took a long pull of the beer the bartender had set in front of him. "Until today, I thought I wouldn't be happy until

Marlene was gone again, but I've been at Jeb's place. Marlene is the only person Wendy has left."

"And what does this have to do with me." He knew he was being obnoxious, but the beer was doing the talking, and he was happy to let it.

"Marlene has changed. She'd never have given up her plans to help anyone before, especially not a kid that didn't have anything to give in return."

"And you're telling me this because?" Bose's head was foggy. Micah's words seemed to be wandering all over the place, and he was having trouble making sense of what the man was saying.

"I pushed Cary away because I didn't believe she was who she appeared to be. Could have been the biggest mistake of my life. Believe me, when I went after her, I was scared shit-less. If I'd have given in to my fear of getting hurt again, I'd have missed out on a loving wife and a great step-mother for Willa and mom for Rodie."

Bose stood, but had to catch hold of the edge of the bar to steady himself. The room twirled around him in a dizzying dance. He plopped back down.

"I'm done preaching, and you're done drinking," Micah said. "I'll take you home, and you can figure out how to get your truck tomorrow."

Bose hadn't had more than a couple of beers since his high school senior party. He'd thought he'd learned that lesson but good. Apparently, he'd been wrong.

The ride home was a blur. Micah sat watching long enough to make sure he made it in the front door. As he collapsed onto his worn leather couch, he saw the headlights flash through the window as the rancher left.

A vision of the redhead swam before his eyes. He slammed them shut. "Not in love with you."

# CHAPTER ELEVEN

Cary took Willa home at eleven o'clock that evening much to the girl's unending complaints. Wendy had put up almost as much of a fight about going to bed, but she hadn't been able to stay awake for more than five minutes after Marlene turned off the light in her room.

Micah insisted on staying until morning.

His presence had given Marlene an opportunity to apologize to her ex-husband. He was a good man, and she'd been too wrapped up in finding money to see it at the time.

Not that she could take any credit for it, but she'd picked a great man to be the father to her daughter.

Other than the apology, they hadn't talked about personal things. Micah had told her what Willa and Rodie had been up to, and she'd filled him in on the sanitized version of her last four years.

As he prepared to leave, he hesitated. "What caused the change in you?"

It was the end of a long night, before she'd had enough coffee, and she didn't have complete control of her brain. She opened her mouth to give him a fluff answer, and Jerry's story spilled out.

"About a year and a half ago, I met a man. I know what you're thinking, but he wasn't my usual type. He was gay. He needed someone so he could appear straight, and I was running out of money." She hesitated. She'd kept Jerry's secret until now. But Jerry was gone, and maybe she'd carried her guilt long enough.

"Go on."

"I loved Jerry, and funny enough, he loved me. We were at a fund-raiser for St Mary's Children's Home. I was helping get bids on the auction, so I was being nice to one of the guys with a big checkbook. He thought a smile bought him handling rights. I could have taken care of the jerk by myself. As you probably know, I have before. But this time, Jerry thought I needed his help." Every painful minute of that night was burned into her brain. If only . . .

But, she'd been *if onlying* herself since the day it happened.

The memory of Jerry jumping off the stage and rushing toward them made her wince. "The man was twice Jerry's size." A vision of the pool of blood on the cement hit like a slug to her chest. She paused to clear her throat. "The guy's punch sent Jerry flying backwards. He hit his head on a cement planter. They got him to a hospital right away, and he had the best doctors, but the damage was done."

"I'm sorry." Micah rose and walked to the kitchen. He brought each of them back a fresh cup of coffee then sat down without saying a word.

The scene played out in her mind like a movie. The anger on Jerry's face as he'd confronted the man, the sight of the jerk running away after, the flash of the ambulance lights. Worst of all, the desolation of standing beside the emergency room bed while Jerry took his last breath.

Marlene took a big swallow of the hot coffee and felt the burn all the way to her stomach. She bit her bottom lip and waited for the wave of emotional pain to recede. "Me, too. Jerry was a good man."

She set her cup on the side table and walked to the

window. Bomber stood with a hip cocked, her eyes closed. Thank goodness the mare was okay. She turned back to find Micah watching her. "His family said I was a gold digger, and they were right, I guess. I just know I was happy with Jerry. I think he was happy with me." In her mind she saw Jerry, his crooked smile and perpetually mussed hair and smiled. "I decided to live the rest of my life the way Jerry saw me. It's a struggle sometimes."

To her surprise, Micah hugged her. "I'll stay with Wendy. You go see if Bose made it through the night. It was touch and go when I left him at his house."

"You didn't tell me you saw Bose last night. Is he hurt?" Marlene flipped her coat off the hook by the front door and stuffed her arms into the sleeves. She hurried through the house searching for her purse. When she came back into the living room, Micah stood by the door smiling.

"He had a battle with demon drink, and I'm pretty sure he lost."

She frowned. "Bose doesn't drink much."

"Neither did I except when I was trying to convince myself I didn't need Cary." He had the self-satisfied smirk of a man who'd battled against love until it won.

Marlene pumped the gas pedal on her old truck several times before turning the key. "Come on. I need you to act like a truck that runs, just for today." She waited a moment and tried again. On the third try, the engine caught, and she gave it a pat on the dashboard. "That's my boy."

Bose's rental was only a few miles from her house, and it only took minutes to get there. She turned off the key and watched as the first rays of the sun peeked over the horizon. The windows were all dark. He'd probably prefer she leave him alone with his hangover, but worry pushed her out of the truck and up the steps.

After knocking several times, she waited another few minutes before giving up and hurrying around to the back. She'd never been to Bose's house before. There were no barns or sheds on the property, no place for him to be besides inside.

She rapped on the back door and when he didn't answer, she pounded. As she started back to the front, her worry growing with every minute, she heard a groan.

"What are you trying to do, knock this house down?" Bose stood in the doorway, dressed in the same clothes he'd had on yesterday. His hair stood on end. One eye was still closed and the other only half open.

She'd always thought sickly green was only an expression. This morning, Bose proved it was a fact. "You look like shit."

"Thanks, I needed that. What do you want?" He held to the edge of the door like it was a life vest in a storm tossed sea.

"I came to tell you Bomber is okay." Marlene gently pushed him inside and closed the door. She left him standing in the pantry and sauntered into the kitchen. "This is a nice little place. How much is the rent?"

"Like that couldn't wait until a decent hour. Do you even know what time it is?" Bose grabbed the coffee carafe. He held it under the faucet and turned the water on. "And what does my rent have to do with anything?"

"It would fill faster if you opened the lid." She took carafe from him and filled the glass pot. "I took Jeb's trailer off the market. I thought I might rent it out."

He slumped into a chair and held his head in his hands. "Thought you needed the money."

Marlene spooned coffee grounds into the basket and soon the aroma of caffeine filled the small kitchen. "I got a job at the café. Cary's friend is willing to take a chance on me. Hope I don't wreck her business."

She snuck a cup of coffee from the coffee maker before it was done and slid it under his nose. A search in his fridge found bacon, eggs, and a several-day-old baked potato.

By the time she had the meal done, she realized Bose

had lifted his head. He watched her as he inhaled the coffee. She poured him another cup and dished up the eggs. "This will help. At least, it always helped me when I drank too much."

Bose poked at the egg and glanced at her with bloodshot eyes. "What makes you think I'm hungover? Maybe I have the flu." He cut off a miniscule piece of egg and put it into his mouth.

She didn't bother to answer his question. With all the drama of the last twelve hours, she'd forgotten to eat dinner. She took a bite of the crispy bacon. This really was good.

"Thanks." He was steady enough to grab the coffeepot and refill their cups before setting it on the table. "But why are you here?"

"Micah said you might need some help this morning. He didn't give me any details, but it looks like you tried to drink the bar dry." She watched as he soaked up the egg yolk with a piece of toast.

"I might have had one too many." Even bloodshot, his dark brown eyes were filled with warmth.

Life's lessons were tough when you were stupid. Ditching Bose was the most idiotic thing in a life filled with selfish moves. "I wanted to make sure you were still alive. I'll be going now."

When he didn't answer, she figured she'd worn out her welcome. She gathered both plates and set them in the sink to soak. "Take care." Her hand reached toward his head before she snatched it back and hurried to her truck. She'd made enough of a fool of herself without letting him know she loved him with all her heart.

She drove on auto pilot all the way home. What the hell she'd thought she could accomplish by going over there, she couldn't figure out. Her hope that Bose would change his mind came to a quick end. She'd even watched her rearview mirror as she'd driven away, but he'd made his position clear when she'd first returned to East Hope.

He might be willing to be friends, but he didn't want a wife and daughter.

As she pulled up to her house, she saw Micah and Wendy sitting on the front steps. She waved as she approached. "It's cold out here. What are you two doing?"

"Waiting for you. Is Bose okay?" Wendy's brows were drawn down and her lips thinned in worry. "I woke up, and Mr. West said you'd gone to help him."

Marlene sat beside Wendy and ruffled her hair. "He's fine. I wanted to thank him for helping us yesterday."

Wendy's face crinkled in disbelief, and she shook her head. "At six in the morning?"

God, she loved this kid. "I'm an early riser."

"No, you're not." Wendy stood and eyed Marlene. "What's going on?"

"You two don't need me to have this conversation, so I'm going home and see what Willa and Rodie are tearing up now." He smiled at Marlene. "Take care, Marlene, and if you need anything . . . Well, you know the drill."

"Thanks." Marlene watched as Micah drove away then she turned to Wendy. "Let's go check Bomber."

"Mr. West and I already checked her."

Marlene took Wendy's hand. "Then walk with me. We have some talking to do.

\*~\*

It had been a week since Marlene had cooked Bose breakfast, and misery had dogged his every step. At first he'd blamed it on the hangover from hell, but as the days went on, he found he couldn't get back into the swing of things.

He wasn't lonely. Well, maybe a little bit. He'd gotten used to dropping by Marlene's every day and seeing her and Wendy. The two times he'd been there this week they hadn't been home.

He was at Mrs. Bouler's ranch attempting to shoe her

fractious four-year-old when his cell rang. The readout on his phone read Gold Medal Dressage.

His dream job was finally calling.

"Bose, it's John Freeman. We've finally got the paperwork through all the channels and if you want the job, it's yours."

He'd been waiting for this news for over a month. When he'd put in his application, he'd toured the facility. It was state of the art, catering to rich owners, top-of-the-line trainers, and million-dollar horses. He should feel more excited.

"You there, Bose?"

"Yeah, I'm here. Just surprised, is all. I'd kind of given up on hearing from you." Bose stepped away from the horse and its octogenarian owner and walked around the corner of the barn. "When do you want me there?"

"Yeah, sorry it took so long. There's lots of red tape on a place like this." The voice crackled out, and Bose moved to clear the connection. "The current farrier will be here until the end of the month, but you can come down sooner if you want."

He thanked Freeman, ended the call, and sank down on a bale of hay beside the barn wall.

"You gonna sit there all day? I need my horse. I got work to do." Mrs. Bouler stood with her hands on her boney hips, glaring at him. Jeb had warned him about this old spitfire. She'd ruled the roost on her husband's ranch since 1940 when they'd gotten married. Since the day he'd died suddenly in the 70s, Ethyl Bouler had run the place by herself and showed no signs of slowing down.

"Got an offer for a job in California." He followed her back to where the gelding stood with his ears laid back, a foot cocked, ready to kick if Bose wasn't careful. Colts like this one made him rethink his decision to shoe horses for a living.

Mrs. Bouler continued to eye him. "Great, finish my gelding before you leave. I gotta use him to gather cattle tomorrow."

"If the stories I've heard are right, you left a rich family back East to marry Mr. Bouler and work this ranch." He knew he was standing onto thin ice questioning the old woman. She was about as secretive as Howard Hughes. "Why?"

"Loved him. Now get to work." She backed toward a pitchfork leaning against the wall. This old gal was as cantankerous as the horses she rode.

Bose decided he'd asked enough questions for today.

He finished the colt and turned him into a pen beside the barn. As he lifted his anvil into the back of his truck, he realized he might be doing this type of shoeing for the last time. No more traveling, no more heaving one hundred pounds of iron into the back of his truck. As soon as he got to California, he'd have a top of the line set-up and people would bring their horses to him.

Rolling his shoeing apron into a neat bundle, he stowed it in its spot in the back of the truck then scanned the area to make sure he had everything. When he looked up, he saw Mrs. Bouler hurrying toward him as fast as her arthritic legs would carry her.

"Brought you your money." She held out a check.

"You usually send it." Bose tucked it into his wallet and looked up to see her holding out a picture frame. "What's this?"

"Harold. In his younger days. Wasn't he something?"

Bose saw a tall, skinny man with a handlebar moustache and a bird's beak nose, dressed in jeans that were a couple of inches too short and high-heeled buckaroo boots. "Yes, ma'am, he was."

"He was a bad 'un when he was younger. My folks hated him, and most everyone around this area told me to stay away from him, but I watched him nurse a litter of two-week old mongrel pups when their mama got hit on the road. That right there tells you somethin' about a person. We were married thirty-four years and still would be if he hadn't got rolled on by a crazy bronc." She touched the picture with one finger then snatched it from his hand. "Don't you got nothin' to do but stand here and waste my time?"

He looked at her, and for the first time since he'd met her, he gave her a genuine smile. "I might not see you again. You take care."

She winked at him. "As sorry a horseshoer as you are, you'll be back. Got to. Ain't nobody but you and old Jeb will put up with me, and he sure as heck can't come shoe my horses from the grave."

She turned on her heel and hobbled back toward the house. When Bose called out his goodbyes, Mrs. Bouler waved over her shoulder and continued on without a word.

Fall had arrived a few days earlier, cloaked in its colorful splendor. Crisp air had replaced the stuffy heat of summer. As he drove away from the H-hanging-B, Bose rolled down the window of his truck. The scent of Juniper and dust filled the cab. An antelope bounded over the fence, disappearing into the desert as he passed the turnoff for the John and June Carter's Bar C Ranch.

He'd met a lot of good people since taking over Jeb's business. He'd met a few difficult ones, too. A mental picture of Mrs. Bouler popped into his head, and he had to smile.

The ranchers and business owners of East Hope were a friendly bunch for the most part, and he loved the wide-open spaces of eastern Oregon. Could a fancy place in California be better than this? He wouldn't know if he didn't check it out.

Besides, it was too late to have second thoughts. He was packed and ready to leave in the morning. Putting off his departure wouldn't make leaving any easier. One more night here, and he'd be on to his dream job.

By the time he'd gotten back to town, he'd talked himself into dropping by Marlene's to say a final good-bye to Wendy. A slight uneasiness itched beneath his skin. What if they were gone? What if he didn't get to see either one of them again?

A rush of relief flowed through him at the sight of Marlene's truck in the driveway, and he had a flash of inspiration. He'd take them with him. If Marlene and Wendy came to California, he wouldn't be lonely. He'd have the best of both worlds.

Wendy ran down the steps and flew into his arms. "Where have you been? I've been watching for you." She took his hand and led him to the house. "Marlene missed you, too."

Marlene sat at the table, sheer pink and white material spread out in front of her. She looked his way then refocused on the dress she was working on. "Hey, Bose."

He almost laughed out loud. Marlene sewing? Now he'd seen everything. "I have some news."

Wendy's eyes brightened, but Marlene didn't respond.

"I got a call from the dressage stables, and they've offered me the job." He watched as the excitement drained from Wendy's eyes.

"Congratulations. You'll do well." Marlene couldn't have made her voice more emotionless if she'd tried for a week. She strung a bead onto a long needle and sewed it onto Wendy's dress.

"I'm leaving tomorrow, but I've had a great idea." He waited until Marlene looked up. "I want you both to come with me."

Marlene returned her gaze to the sewing. She wove the needle into the cloth then carefully folded the garment. Swiveling in the chair, she watched him with suspicious eyes. "If you're asking me to marry you, you're doing a crappy job of it."

Her question hit him with the force of a cannon ball. He'd never considered marriage. He just didn't want to leave Marlene and Wendy. He sat straighter and looked from Wendy to Marlene. "No. I want you two to come to

California with me."

Marlene stood, her face a mask of disappointment. Her brittle smile looked like it would crack apart any minute. "Thank you for the offer, but we'll have to decline. Without looking away, she said, "Wendy, would you go do something with the horses? Please."

Wendy looked from him to Marlene then got up without a word and left.

When he looked back at Marlene, her emotionless expression changed to fury. "You don't love either one of us enough to be a family, but you don't want to be lonesome, is that it? I might not deserve more, but Wendy does."

# CHAPTER TWELVE

Bose hadn't slept well during the night. He'd had the gooseneck trailer hooked up and was pulling out of the driveway before first light. At Jeb's place, he caught Louie and loaded the gelding. He'd written a generous check for the roan and left it in Marlene's mailbox. The compulsion to take something from East Hope was strong, and since Marlene and Wendy wouldn't go, the colt was the next best thing.

The drive to Reno normally took a little over six hours. A flat on the trailer in the middle of nowhere along with the wrong sized lug wrench, guaranteed he'd arrive late. The only bright spot in a day from hell was the man who stopped to help. He'd be forever grateful to the trucker.

The Livestock center had been deserted, and he'd spent too long scaring up someone to unlock a stall. His eyes had felt like someone had thrown sand in them, and he'd ached from head to toe.

When he unloaded Louie, the blue roan jigged beside him, nickering, searching for his friend.

"Lonesome for Bomber?" Bose hung a hay net inside the stall and filled Louie's water bucket. "I am, too."

A cloud of dust had puffed up as he'd dropped onto

the mattress he'd thrown into the gooseneck of his trailer several months ago. The plan had been to go elk hunting. Like all his plans of late, that hadn't worked out. Pulling off his boots and coat, he'd climbed into his sleeping bag.

Worries about whether he was doing the right thing combined with Louie's lonesome whinnies kept him from getting a wink of sleep. After hours of tossing and turning, Bose had had enough. He fed Louie early, and by the time the sun rose, he'd loaded the gelding, packed up the few things he'd gotten out, and climbed into the driver's seat.

A convenience store at the edge of town had passable coffee and a great selection of donuts. He ate while he fueled up the rig then refilled his coffee cup for the trip. Walking to the trailer, he looked in on Louie. The colt nickered. "For good or bad, we're on to a new adventure, buddy."

A few puffy clouds wandered across the bright blue sky. Traffic was light, and Bose hummed along with Trace Atkins as he sang about wanting to feel something. He pounded out the beat to Tim McGraw's *Better Than I Used To Be* with his fingers against the steering wheel. When Montgomery Gentry came on singing *Some People Change*, he'd had enough, and he switched off the radio.

At noon, and even though he didn't feel the least bit hungry, he stopped. Louie needed to get out and move around. He led the gelding enough to stretch his legs then tied him to the trailer. "Wish we could find someplace to turn you out for a while, but this will have to do. Only a few more hours."

An overcooked burger and a watery coke was the best he could get in the one-horse town, and as soon as he'd finished, he loaded Louie back up and headed down the highway.

The longer he drove, the more his stomach complained. Greasy food was no match for the great cook Marlene had become.

After the mess with Marlene when he was young, he'd gone out of his way to stay away from drama. The last few weeks had been filled with more chaos and sorrow than he'd ever seen, but with one decision, he'd swept it all away. At least he'd tried.

He settled into the drive and let his imagination take wing. The hours behind the wheel gave him time to think. Should he give up what he really wanted to stay locked into a plan he'd made years ago? The decision he made might not be the most financially lucrative, but it was the right one.

He slowed the rig to twenty-five miles an hour as he pulled into East Hope. The familiar sights calmed his nerves, and when he pulled into Marlene's driveway, he knew he was home. Now all he had to do was convince her she needed him as much as he needed her and Wendy.

After pulling behind the mobile home, he unloaded Louie. The gelding was going crazy talking to his friend. Bomber stood at the gate, answering the colt.

At the ruckus, Wendy came running out. "Where have you been? Marlene said you'd left for good." The girl's eyes were big as he handed her the gelding's rope.

"I needed to figure some things out, and I did. Will you put Louie away? I have to talk to Marlene." When Wendy nodded, he turned for the house. Time to ante up.

Marlene stood at the sink pretending she wasn't watching him out the window. When he entered the house, she focused all her attention on the head of lettuce she was washing.

"I need to talk to you."

He might as well have been invisible and mute.

"Marlene, I . . ."

She looked up, tears streaming down her face.

The Marlene he knew didn't cry. When he tried to pull her into his arms, she jerked away from his grasp.

"Don't mess with Wendy and me." There was a growl in her voice like a mother tiger on the fight.

"I'm not, I—"

She cut him off with a wave of her hand. "If it had been just me when you asked us to go to California, I'd have beat you to the truck. But it isn't. I need to make a stable home for Wendy, and it has to be here. This is where she lived with her dad, and she's not ready to leave yet." Her voice hitched, and she stared into the sink.

He dropped his hands to his sides and waited while she regained her composure.

She wiped the tears away, took a deep breath and faced him.

Her beautiful blue gaze shot straight to his soul, and all his doubts disappeared. If it took until he was eighty, he'd win her back.

"I know I'm the last person who should get to say your leaving is wrong, but I'm saying it. I know I hurt you by marrying Micah, but I never knew how deep. There's no way I can make it up to you other than to promise I won't do anything like that again."

When he started to talk, she held up her hand. "Wendy isn't ready to leave East Hope, and I'll stay here until she is."

"Marlene." She continued to scrub the lettuce. Bose waited until curiosity won out and she glanced at him. "I'm not leaving East Hope either. Ever. I'm staying right here, and we'll figure this out, but I need you to do me one favor."

"What?"

"Please stop killing that poor head of lettuce."

She looked at her hands and the bits of green that were stuck to her fingers before raising her gaze to meet his. "Do you mean you'll stay here and help me raise Wendy?"

"I'll live here with you and Wendy as long as that is what you want. I'll move with you if Wendy wants to move. I'll do anything you think is best."

She stiffened then turned to him, her fingers clutching the tattered head of lettuce, her face pinched as if she were preparing for the worst.

"I've been thinking about what you said before about marriage. If I'm not in this all the way, it won't work. I'm asking you to be my wife." Bose held his breath and crossed his fingers for luck.

Good thing there was a chair behind Marlene because she sank onto the seat without looking. He'd expected her to be thrilled. He couldn't imagine what she was thinking, but she didn't look happy.

"You think you can waltz in here and ask me to marry you, and I'll fall down at your feet in gratitude?"

"No, I thought you'd agree, possibly give me a mind-altering kiss then we'd get married, and if Wendy wants to, we'd adopt her. What's wrong with that?"

"I think you've made a spur of the moment decision because you feel guilty about leaving Wendy." Her expression was hard, angry and desolate. She walked to the door and opened it. "You need to go."

Bose walked across the room until he was directly in front of Marlene. He reached out to touch her cheek, but when she flinched he dropped his arm to his side. This was harder than he'd figured.

Marlene straightened. She tucked her fingers into her front pockets and rocked back on her heels. "I've worked hard to become a better person, and in the process I've realized I deserve more than someone's scraps. I'm not going to take anyone's leftovers."

This time Bose didn't back off. He placed a palm on each cheek and looked into her eyes. "I love you, Marlene. I've loved you since the first time I saw you. Whether you believe me or not, my love isn't going to change."

Marlene didn't answer, but she didn't move away, so he rushed on. "I'm going to ask you once again to marry me and if you say no, I'll ask you again tomorrow. I'll ask the next day and the next week and the next month." He leaned forward and touched his lips to hers before looking into her eyes. "Marlene Clegg, will you be my wife?" He held his breath. He talked big, but he didn't know what he'd do if she turned him down.

"You really want to marry me?" Her eyes were narrowed in suspicion.

He nodded.

"You love me?" Her breath hitched on the last word.

"Yes, more than Little Louie loves his grain."

A tentative smile spread across her lovely face, and then a sweet laugh burst from her lips. She reached out and placed her palm against his cheek. "How could any girl turn down a sweet talker like you?"

A loud whoop interrupted Marlene and echoed through the house. Wendy pushed the door all the way open as she rushed in. "I didn't think you were ever going to say yes. Do I get to be the flower girl?"

As they pulled Wendy into a three-way hug, Bose kissed her on the top of the head.

Marlene knelt and touched the girl's face. "No, you're not going to be the flower girl." At Wendy's crestfallen look, Marlene hurried on. "You're going to be my Maid of Honor, and Willa is going to walk me down the aisle."

# EPILOGUE

Five weeks later—

When Marlene had first imagined marrying Bose, the wedding she'd mentally planned had been a small affair, shared with only Bose's parents, Gran and Uncle Jeb.

She peeked out the dressing room door at the filled-to-capacity East Hope Methodist Church.

The whole town was here. It was only minutes before the start of the ceremony, and she was battling a bad case of matrimonial nerves when she heard the outside door open. Turning, she saw Millie Barnes enter the room.

"This is the last thing I need," she groaned. Not on her wedding day. Most of the rest of the town had taken Micah and Cary's word that she'd changed. She didn't get dirty looks when she walked down the street, and Cary and Pansy had even given her a small shower.

Millie had been invited but hadn't attended.

Marlene could do without the storeowner's friendship, but it made her sad that such an important East Hope citizen still hated her. She straightened. She'd let Millie have her say then try to forget the harsh words. And, they would be harsh she had no doubt.

Marlene smoothed the fitted waist of dress and

prepared to meet Millie head on. Pansy Vaughn had loaned her a 1950s, powder blue halter dress, and Cary had loaned her a pair of white pumps. She had the blue and borrowed things down pat. Her underwear was new. She and Cary had driven to Bend where Marlene had splurged at the mall lingerie shop.

Bose was going to love her latest purchases.

Millie had stopped in the middle of the floor, her gaze sweeping the room as she moved closer to Marlene.

"Cary and Pansy already went to sit down. If you're looking for them, you're too late."

Millie tilted her head and smiled. "I'm not looking for those two. I'm looking for the bride."

"Look, Millie. I know you have no intention of forgiving me, but this is my wedding day. Please don't screw it up." Might as well be up front with the woman. Being nice hadn't helped. "I love Bose, and I won't hurt him or Willa again. What can I do to make you believe me?"

Millie walked a slow circle around Marlene, looking her up and down. When she reached the front, she stopped. "I have something for you."

"Not a punch in the nose, I hope." Marlene tried to laugh, but she wasn't absolutely sure Millie wouldn't take a swing at her.

Millie held out a small, white jeweler's box. "Cary told me you needed something old. Will this do?"

Marlene lifted off the top to find an antique pearl necklace nestled in a bed of cotton. She reached in a finger and stroked one of the creamy pearls. "These are—." She cleared the tears from her throat. "These are beautiful, but I couldn't."

Jerking the box out of Marlene's hands, Millie reached in and pulled out the necklace. "Turn around." The pearls settled warm and beautiful around Marlene's neck.

Millie closed the clasp then turned Marlene to face her. "These were my grandmother's. She was married for sixty-one years. I wore them at both of my weddings, and I've had good marriages."

"But, you don't even like me," Marlene blurted out. Millie's kind action had her flustered. "I don't know what to say."

"Don't be a twit. Wear the pearls." Millie's grin took the sting out of her words. "Besides, if you screw up the something old, new, borrowed and blue adage, the marriage gods will take revenge. Bose will have a beer belly before you've been married a year. I'm doing this as much for him as for you."

Marlene grabbed a tissue from the box and blotted her eyes. Seemed like crying was her go-to emotion lately. "Where's my bouquet?"

As Millie tipped up the lid of the florist's box, pine scent wafted out.

The small shop on the edge of East Hope had made a special bouquet of Sugar Pine boughs, pinecones and white roses. Marlene bit the inside of her cheek to keep the tears at bay. Geez, she needed to open a water works.

Millie placed the pine bouquet in Marlene's arms. Holding her at arms length, the older woman smiled. "One word of advice. Don't you screw this up."

Before Marlene could thank Millie, Willa opened the door. "Come on, Mom. You're going to be late."

Stepping out into the hallway, Marlene hesitated as she surveyed the church. Willa and Wendy wore similar dark blue dresses, and Rodie, in a tiny suit, had dropped piles of white rose petals all along the aisle.

In her dreams Marlene's weddings had either been tiny and intimate or over-the-top extravagant. Never something as perfect as this, in a hometown church, surrounded by friends.

She felt a gentle push against the small of her back. "Get a move on girl," Millie whispered. "Or some other woman will gather up that gorgeous hunk of man, and you'll lose out."

Peace settled over Marlene as she looked down the aisle to Bose then from Willa to Wendy. Flashes of jealousy between the girls had made for some interesting times, but on the whole, her life couldn't have been better.

Marlene turned to Willa. "I'll be just a moment." She closed her eyes and bowed her head before whispering a missive to her uncle. "Jeb, I owe this all to you. You thought you were leaving me a house, and you really left me a life filled with love."

She smiled to herself as the first notes of Mendelssohn's Wedding March filled the air.

"Oh, and Wendy says to say thanks, too. The money from the sale of your medical marijuana is now in her college fund."

*~*

The five months leading up to the finalization of Wendy's adoption were tension filled. There were more home visits and paperwork than Marlene thought possible. She gotten to the point where she was afraid to give anyone an opinion on even the mildest subject for fear she'd say something wrong and mess up the proceedings. Thank goodness she had Bose to talk her down when the stress became too much.

The blocky, three-story building that housed the Harney County Courthouse was unassuming, but within those red brick walls was the key to happiness. She followed Wendy up the wide cement steps toward the heavy, glass doors, her heart stuck in her throat.

It had taken five months and a week to get their final meeting before the judge, and Marlene hadn't totally relaxed the whole time. If Family Court denied their petition to adopt Wendy, she didn't know what she'd do.

After all the worry and agonizing they'd gone through waiting for this day, the actual process was over in minutes. When the judge finally said Wendy was officially

Wendy Wilson-Kovac, the three of them danced around the courtroom. The court officials weren't impressed, but the citizens of East Hope who'd come to celebrate Wendy's adoption joined in with whoops and cheers.

Horns honked as the cars and trucks made a caravan all the way back to Jeb's place.

Bose parked in back and Wendy jumped out. "I'm going to tell Bomber."

Bose and Marlene had made it almost to the back door when they heard Wendy scream. They found her down by the creek. She stood stock still, but she vibrated with excitement.

"Look, you guys! Bomber had her colt! She got a new family the same day I did."

Marlene stood back and watched as Bose approached the mare. He ran his hand down Bomber's neck. The baby watched him, not quite sure of this new creature in her life. "It's a filly."

Wendy stood on the other side of the mare, trying to peek beneath her belly to see the baby. The buttermilk buckskin filly wobbled around her mama's butt and stopped, staring at the girl. Wendy turned to face them, her eyes shining. "She's so pretty. Oh, Bose. Isn't she just the prettiest little thing?"

Before he could answer, Wendy called out. "Willa! Willa, come see what Bomber has."

Willa raced across the pasture to stand beside Wendy. "We've got a lot of broodmares on the Circle W, but there isn't a colt on our place that's as nice as this one." Willa put her arm around Wendy's waist. "What are you going to name her?"

"I like Fine French Dining, but she belongs to Bose."

"Frenchy it is." Bose took his arm from around Marlene's shoulders. He smiled at the girls. "Let's leave Bomber alone for a while and go get something to eat."

As Bose and the girls walked toward the house discussing the new addition to the herd, Marlene stayed a few steps behind, watching them in wonder. She had more than she'd ever known existed, friends, a home, and the biggest gift of all, a family.

Whether luck was made or given didn't matter to her.

Somehow she'd become the luckiest woman in the world.

*

***Dear Reader,***
***If you've got a moment, Marlene and Bose would love for you to leave a review.***

## _Romance Beneath A Rodeo Moon_

If you enjoyed reading Sugar Pine Cowboy, you can find the cowboys and cowgirls of East Hope, Oregon in the Sugar Coated Cowboys series. Begin with Cary and Micah's story in *Gimme Some Sugar.*

http://amzn.to/1UDCemK

**Gimme Some Sugar**-Book 1, Sugar Coated Cowboys series

Pastry chef, Cary Crockett, is on the run. Pursued by a loan shark bent on retrieving gambling debts owed him by her deadbeat ex-boyfriend, she finds the perfect hiding place at the remote Circle W Ranch. More at home with city life, cupcakes and croissants than beef, beans and bacon, she has to convince ranch owner Micah West she's up to the job of feeding his hired hands. The overwhelming attraction she feels toward him was nowhere in the job description.

Micah West has a big problem. The camp-cook on his central Oregon ranch has up and quit without notice,

and his crew of hungry cowboys is about to mutiny. He agrees to hire Cary on a temporary basis, just until he finds the right man to fill the job. Maintaining a hands-off policy toward his sexy new cook becomes tougher than managing a herd of disgruntled wranglers.
http://amzn.to/1UDCemK

## Gimme Some Sugar Excerpt

Snapping his head up, he whirled around, almost elbowing the woman standing behind him. Pulling in a deep, slow breath, partly to gather some semblance of calm and partly to adjust to the tingle where her hand met his arm, he took a step back before speaking.

"Help me with what?" Did he know her? He was sure he didn't, but man….

"I'm sorry. I didn't mean to eavesdrop, but I heard you say you're looking for a cook." Golden eyes the color of whiskey stared into his. "I cook."

He let his gaze wander over her, liking what he saw. She wasn't a local. Her white blond hair was as short as a man's on the sides and curled longer on the top and back. He hadn't seen any woman, or anyone at all who wore their hair like this. Of course, tastes of the people of East Hope ran to the conservative.

Despite the severe hairstyle, she was pretty. Beyond pretty. Leather pants showed off her soft curves, miniature combat boots encased her small feet and a tight tank top enhanced her breasts.

When she cleared her throat, he jerked his eyes up to her face. "It won't do you any good to talk to my breasts. Like most women, it's my brain that answers questions."

A smart ass and she'd caught him red-handed. His cheeks warmed. Damn it, he was blushing. This woman was not at all what he needed. Time to end this. "I have a ranch, the Circle W. We need a camp cook. A man."

Her eyes narrowed, and her body tensed. "It looks like

you need any kind of cook you can get." She held her hand out, indicating the empty café. "Not a lot of takers."

She had him there. His gut told him he was going to regret this, but she was right. He had no choice. "I'll hire you week to week." When she nodded, he continued. "I've got seven ranch hands. You'll cook breakfast and dinner and pack lunches, Monday through Friday and serve Sunday dinner to the hands who are back by six o'clock."

She bounced on the toes of her feet until she noticed him watching her then she pulled on a cloak of calm indifference. "You won't regret this."

He felt a smile touch the corners of his mouth as his gut twisted. "I already do."

http://amzn.to/1UDCemK

https://amzn.to/2te3VOt

**Sweet Cowboy Kisses**-Book 2, Sugar Coated Cowboys series

To attain his dream of becoming a World Champion bull-rider, Kade Vaughn must ride the bad one they call Swamp Fox. But in two previous rides, the big bull's given

Kade two disqualifications and a severe concussion. Now the cowboy's on a forced vacation at his friends' ranch, near the little town of East Hope, Oregon. It's all fine and dandy till the day he walks into the diner and comes face to face with a temptress in a Cleopatra wig. One who looks a lot like the girl he left behind, and who he'd give nearly anything to have back in his arms.

To get through each day, Pansy Lark pretends to be other women through cosplay--famous, strong women who took what they wanted from life, instead of the other way around. Once she was a champion barrel racer with a bright future, and a cowboy she loved. She lost it all, leaving her with the driving need to prove she's not that weak girl anymore. But when Kade walks back into her life, she must decide if real strength is in forgiveness.

Can sweet cowboy kisses heal her wounded heart?
https://amzn.to/2te3VOt

## Sweet Cowboy Kisses Excerpt

Chancing a look into his eyes, ready to tell him to leave, she stopped. He didn't recognize her, the bastard.

To his credit—if she was forced to give him any kind of positive acknowledgement—she was about as far from the dutiful little cowgirl of her younger years as possible. And thank goodness for that.

She didn't need a stroll down a painful memory lane right now.

Seven years ago, she'd abandoned the life she'd had in Montana. She hadn't wanted to leave her horses and the thrill of running barrels, but when Kade left her and her overbearing father asked the impossible, she'd fled and not looked back.

The day her father urged her to get an abortion was too much. Leaving the things she loved behind, Pansy had changed every detail possible about herself, including her clothing, personality and possibly her thoughts. She'd become the epitome of a city girl.

"What can I get you?" She stepped farther into the room and folded her arms across her chest. She hadn't seen Kade in seven years and seeing him today was about twenty years too soon. It had taken her forever to see the man as he really was, certainly not someone she could count on. He was tumbleweed, a wanderer, who was happy to let life blow him to his next adventure.

He tilted his head as he looked at her. His eyebrows lifted as he took in the soft folds of her white dress.

She'd made this replica of the gown Liz Taylor wore in Cleopatra, and it was one of her favorites.

Then he raised his gaze to her gold trimmed black wig and overly made-up eyes.

For a moment, she thought he might see beyond the costume to who she really was. That moment was gone before she could blink.

With a slight shake of his head, he broke eye contact and grabbed a menu from the stand. "I'll have the breakfast special, eggs over easy and the bacon just this side of burnt."

A jolt of unease mixed with regret shot through her when his slate gray eyes met hers.

"Oh, and coffee. Lots of coffee."

Pansy nodded then escaped into the kitchen. Of all the small town cafes in all of the western United States, he had to walk into hers. She cracked three eggs onto the griddle beside the pile of fresh grated potatoes and four strips of bacon then dropped the shells one by one into the garbage. The loud ticking of the old school clock above the door competed with the sizzle of the food as it cooked.

Pulling a deep breath into her lungs, she let it out bit by bit. It would be okay. She didn't think Kade recognized her, at least not yet. Hopefully, their past and her pain could stay right where she'd hidden it.

Maybe he was passing through on his way to another

bull riding. If she had an ounce of luck left, he'd be gone as soon as he had breakfast. Pansy grabbed the coffee pot and a mug. Time to play up Pansy Lark, city girl, cosplayer and cook extraordinaire.

"Here you go." She poured the mug full of coffee and placed it before him. Keeping her head down, she let the locks of her wig shadow her face. "Your breakfast will be out in a minute."

"You weren't here the last time I visited East Hope." Kade's deep voice reverberated through her bones. She'd always loved his voice, and his touch, and . . .

Enough! She hurried toward the kitchen door but stopped when she reached it. It would be rude not to answer. If she hadn't been rude all those years ago, she could be polite now. "I've been here about ten months."

"Where you from? Not from around here."

"What makes you say that?" She wasn't going into her personal life. Kade had given up any right to know about her past.

"The hair-do. Don't know many East Hopians who channel Cleopatra—or any woman but a fifties country western singer." The smile he shot her way made her heart do a tap dance around her chest. "Big hair rules in these parts."

https://amzn.to/2te3VOt

https://amzn.to/2JF54tn

**Cowboy's Sweetheart**-Book 3, Sugar Coated Cowboys series

Byron Garrett has found peace as a cowboy on the Circle W ranch. He's far from his controlling father and the man's demands that Byron make him proud as a pro football player. Born a city boy, he's discovered a passion for the land, his horses and the cowboy way of life. He's created the lifestyle he always wanted, and it doesn't include a woman or the complications that come with love. At least, not until a bubbly artist shows up and does her best to tear down the corral he's built around his heart.

Vivi Beckett is searching for a place that feels like home. After traveling the country, she's finally found it in the beautiful wilds of Oregon. With the inheritance left her when she was orphaned, she can buy a place to live and create her art. But after meeting Byron, Vivi suspects her dream alone won't be enough to bring her happiness … not unless he's at her side.

All of Vivi's dreams are at risk when she discovers her inheritance is in jeopardy. She needs help, but will Byron

be willing to join her on a different, and perhaps even better path, and make her a Cowboy's Sweetheart?
https://amzn.to/2JF54tn

## Cowboy's Sweetheart Excerpt

Out of the corner of his eye, he saw movement. A colorful vision floated toward where he sat beside the round pen. Wisps of light, frothy material floated with the woman's movements. Long blonde curls bounced as she ran toward him.

Even the colt stopped bucking to watch her approach. He danced on his toes, ready to run at the slightest provocation.

Byron stood and held out his hand to stop the woman and returned his gaze to the colt.

"Are you okay?" she called, continuing to advance at a slower pace.

He whirled on her. He didn't want to yell. That might be all it would take for Crater to decide leaving was his best option. Luckily, his stare had its intended effect.

She froze in her tracks.

Byron turned back to the animal, crooning in a near whisper as he approached the scared colt. "Don't worry, little man. I won't let the big, bad lady near you." The paint was a bundle of nerves, but he stood until Byron could get a hand on the reins. "Let's get you put away."

He started toward the barn, but felt the change in the gelding the minute something behind them moved. Crater jumped and tried to push past him, slapping Byron in the jaw with his head. Byron took a minute to reassure the colt again, ignoring the pain, before turning to the woman. She'd stopped where she was, but the wind was whipping her skirt around her thighs.

High-heeled knee-high boots were as inappropriate for ranch wear as the rest of her costume.

She looked like a woodland fairy or maybe one of those hippy girls he'd read about from the Seventies.

"Are you okay?" She stayed where she was, but didn't retreat. She hadn't taken his heavy-handed hint to leave. That's why he hung around horses, cats and dogs and not people. Hell, he even preferred hamsters.

If he'd been a friendlier man, he'd have taken a moment to explain why she was scaring the horse, and that he was fine. He could have asked her to leave him alone, but he'd found people rarely believed him if he politely told them he didn't want their company, so he'd quit.

Turning, he led the colt into the barn. He pulled his custom-made Wade saddle off the colt and stowed it in the tack room. He'd special ordered it from Hamley & Co. in Pendleton a few years earlier, and besides the horses he owned, it was one of his most prized possessions.

As he left the stall after turning the colt loose, Byron glanced out the door. The flower child stood where he'd left her, one hand raised, wiggling her fingers at him.

Just what he needed. A hippy do-gooder. She probably loved wolves and spotted owls. Thought they were people with fur and feathers.

It would only take a few minutes to throw a leaf of hay in Crater's manger and make his escape out the other end of the barn.

If he continued to walk away, even this flower child would take the hint that he didn't want her company. Right?

https://amzn.to/2JF54tn

https://amzn.to/2t27KXv

**Changing A Cowboy's Tune**-Book 1, Rodeo Road series

When her fiancé demands Mavis abandon her goal of barrel racing at the National Finals Rodeo, she chooses to follow her dream and loses the man she adores.

Dex wants nothing more than to marry the woman he loves and build a future on his family's ranch, but when he pushes her to settle into life as a mother and rancher's wife, she bolts.

Years apart haven't dampened their desire, but can they see past their own dreams for the future and invent a life they both love?

https://amzn.to/2t27KXv

## Changing A Cowboy's Tune Excerpt

Poor Tuneful blew out a loud snort and danced sideways. Normally a quiet mare, the gray could feel Mavis' nervous tension.

*Get it together.* Mavis hadn't been this nervous at the biggest futurities in the country. She dismounted and led the mare along the arena fence.

Tuneful relaxed, dropping her head as her steps slowed.

When Mavis reached the bucking chutes, she turned toward the entry gate. There was only one more bronc rider then a few ropers before the first barrel racer would be called into the arena. She stepped out of the way as a man hopped over the fence and dropped to the ground in front of her.

"Your run'll be faster if you get on the horse." The deep vibes of a familiar voice sent shock waves through her body. Adrenaline shot spiky prickles down her arms.

Fate must have it in for her. She turned toward the parking lot, away from Dex. Maybe if she pretended she hadn't heard, he'd disappear.

"Been a while, Maple. You're lookin' great."

"Don't call me that," she called over her shoulder, hurrying toward her truck. Footsteps followed her. The only way she'd get away now was to run, and she wasn't giving this cowboy the satisfaction. She pivoted on one foot and turned to see the most beautiful man God had ever created, at least in her eyes.

His smile touched her soul, right up until she remembered the words he'd shouted at her the last time they'd seen each other. "Leave me alone. I said everything I had to say to you six years ago."

"You didn't say anything. You left without a word." For an instant, sadness filled his gaze. He pushed it away with a killer grin as he moved closer. "I'm glad to see you're back."

His unique scent filled the evening air, and the feeling of being in his arms rushed back. On its heels was the memory of his demands. He was crowding her, but she'd be damned if she'd back away. "Why? I haven't changed. You didn't like the way I was before. You won't like me any better now."

The man had a talent for doing the right thing. Except when it came to her. Memories washed over her, and she yanked her thoughts back to the jerk standing beside her horse.

"Oh, I liked you well enough, and you once told me I was perfect." His grin was almost enough to make her drop her defenses. It had been in the past, but not this time.

His soft chuckle touched her mind like a feather in the wind.

Mavis broke eye contact and turned toward the gate. There were only four calf ropers left to compete. She put her foot into the stirrup and swung up on Tuneful. "I'd love to stay and reminisce about the good old days, but my mind's blank at the moment."

She nudged Tuneful's sides with her heels and rode the mare toward the arena.

"I'm here for a while. We'll get together." Dex's voice followed her through the night.

"Not if I can help it." As she muttered the words, a brilliant red pickup with Northwest Auto & Truck emblazoned on the sides carried the three barrels into the arena.

Damn Dex Dunbar!

She'd had six years free of the man. Six years of peace. Six years of not waiting to see which of her dreams he'd try to crush. And now within a day of when she'd arrived home, he'd found her again.

https://amzn.to/2t27KXv

# ABOUT THE AUTHOR

Stephanie Berget was born loving horses, a ranch kid trapped in a city girl's body. It took her twelve years to convince her parents she needed a horse of her own. She found her way to rodeo when she married her own, hot cowboy. She and the Bronc Rider traveled throughout the Northwest while she ran barrels and her cowboy rode bucking horses. She started writing to put a realistic view of rodeo and ranching into western romance. Stephanie and her husband live on a farm, located along the Oregon/Idaho border. They raise hay, horses and cattle, with the help of Dizzy Dottie, the Border Collie and Cisco, barrel and team roping horse extraordinaire.

Stephanie is delighted to hear from readers. Reach her at
http://www.stephanieberget.com
Facebook: https://www.facebook.com/stephaniebergetwrites/
Amazon: Stephanie Berget
Twitter: https://twitter.com/StephanieBerget

STEPHANIE BERGET

# AUTHOR NOTES

Thank you for reading beyond the end of the book and all the way to the author notes. You are the bomb! I stole this line from Craig Martelle. Shhhh! Don't tell him, and we'll all be good. ☺

I had such a good time writing Marlene and Bose's story. Unlike some books, they talked to me all the way through. Marlene worked so hard trying to redeem herself, and I think she accomplished that. And Bose. Who couldn't love him?

I'd also like to thank Liz Mudd and Millie Swank. They've been reading about my Sugar Coated Cowboys since the beginning. I think we need to put them in a book.

Since I'm getting to a point where I don't run barrels much anymore, writing about cowboys and cowgirls is the next best thing. If you have any ideas about future books or characters, shoot me an email. You never know, your ideas might end up in a book.

I appreciate everyone who picks up one of my books and reads it all the way to the end. Thank you for reading my books and I hope you enjoy them. Without you, most of these books wouldn't exist.

Without readers, there is very little reason to keep writing.

Printed in Great Britain
by Amazon